MEMORY FOG

MEM🍋RY FOG

CYNTHIA HOELSCHER

DECANT

First published in 2023 by Decant
An imprint of Decant Books, LLC.
www.decantbooks.com

Hardback ISBN 979-8-9892670-2-6
Paperback ISBN 979-8-9892670-1-9
ebook ISBN 979-8-9892670-0-2

Cover design by Laura Duffy
Library of Congress Control Number: 2023919053
Printed in the United States of America

To Judy and Pete, the heart never forgets.

INTRODUCTION

The life of a family caregiver is one that we often do not hear enough about. The journey of caring for a loved one is a lot of things, isolating, exhausting, confusing, and everything in between. But it can also be beautiful. There are many moments during the dementia journey that are special, and you will keep in your heart forever.

This story gives a voice to the many caregivers that face this journey. The progression of becoming a caregiver varies but one thing is often true, we do not seek out the opportunity to be family caregivers. This role is often thrust upon us. Waking up and realizing you are a caregiver, especially one for an aging parent can be sobering. It is a difficult experience that requires resilience, support, and love.

A common theme I hear from family caregivers is that they feel alone. There are millions of family caregivers in America, alone. The number of family caregivers is growing every day. Memory Fog gives a look inside the storyline that millions are living today. The daily stress and anxiety that being a caregiver adds on top of everything humans endure already is overwhelming. The pressure of caring for another person is heavy. The majority of people do not realize how much goes into caring for another, especially one living with a progressive disease such as dementia.

Unfortunately, our society has not grasped the enormity of this issue quite yet. We are at the brink of a care crisis. This is going to become the reality for more people than we can fathom. This story shines a light on this beautiful yet difficult journey.

Thank you,

Carrie Aalberts M.S., CDP, CMDCP

Founder of Dementia Darling

www.dementiadarling.com

CHAPTER 1

The yellow lab barked every morning. By the time the barking started she could tell if the neighbor was running late or on time to fight the early morning Houston traffic. Pearl, a white Labrador retriever, who could not retrieve anything to save her life, went out habitually before the sun was even thinking of coming up, to take care of her morning business. This morning, Sam was not awakened by the repetitive warning yelps that Pearl usually emitted just to let everyone know that she was still the boss of her backyard domain, but instead, it was a deep, baritone rumbling that seemed to vibrate the walls in her small bedroom.

It took a minute for Sam to orient herself and recognize that what she was listening to was the heartbreaking sound of yet another 1950s-era cottage being demolished. This was becoming a familiar event in the geographically desirable neighborhood where many of the single story, shiplap siding houses were originally sold to World War II veterans and cared for lovingly for generations. Now, the property value far outweighed the structural value. The coveted lots were being cleared to make way for new homes that would certainly include a two story brick or stucco exterior, a game room, walk-in closets, and a wine bar.

She knew that a fellow neighbor in the recently gentrified community would soon complain to the neighborhood authorities that the construction noise was beginning way too early. The Golden Oaks and Oak Forest neighborhoods, or the GOOF, in Houston, Texas, were just one of the communities in the Houston metropolitan area undergoing an urban revival.

Many investors and young prospective homeowners loved the neighborhoods located right outside of the 610 Loop, the main artery around downtown Houston. Others were impressed with the oversized lots that would accommodate three car garages and a swimming pool. Whatever the reason, the GOOF was the latest and greatest place to take up residence.

Sam swung her feet out of her bed and sat up slowly, trying to get her thoughts to mesh and prompt her brain to focus on what her day's schedule was supposed to be. She knew she was one of the lucky ones who did not have to sit at a desk from eight to five every workday, and she was certainly not complaining, but some mornings she just could not come up with where and what she was supposed to be doing. This issue would later give her something to worry about.

She quietly tiptoed to the kitchen on the original stained white oak floors that showed a worn path from her room, down the tiny hall, through the den, and into the kitchen. Sam desperately needed a bump of caffeine, and then she would decide what she was going to do with this little gift of extra time, even if she came to it by way of a noisy John Deere excavator. She was not used to having extra time on her hands, and now that she was up, she was going to carefully consider her options.

Sam thought about backtracking to check her schedule for the day that was neatly recorded in her faithful day planner in her bedroom. With a fluctuating teaching schedule, school classes, homework, and projects, she could only get through each day if she was well organized. Recalling her calendar in her head, she was sure she was free until mid-morning when she was booked to teach her first class, and then a late lunch with her aunt.

Sawyer Anne Martin, or Sam, as any friend or family member called her, walked into the kitchen and noticed the light over the small table was shining. A quick glance at the backdoor indicated that the deadbolt was not engaged. Sam walked over to the coffee pot and started a fresh pot. As she leaned back onto the kitchen counter with her arms crossed and looked around, she knew that she was indeed the first person up in the house on Lamonte Lane. No coffee brewing. No dirty cereal bowl in the sink. No television blaring the morning news. The lights had been left on and the door unlocked from the night before. Again.

Well, I'll be go to hell, she thought to herself. *Is there a Mr. Wonderful that I don't know about, and was Mom hoping he would sneak in through the back door?* And then she thought to herself, *Would that be such a terrible thing? A good daddy might be just what this home needs.*

Her biological father had never been in the picture, and when Sam would venture to ask, her mother was reluctant to go into detail about their time together. Judy often said that he was a good man who wasn't ready to be a father when she got pregnant. According to Judy, he knew about her, and Sam thought he could find *her* if he ever wanted to really be her dad. She also knew they could have been easily *found* if he had had the desire to meet his daughter. It wasn't until recently, though, that she started to realize just how nice it would be to lean on another parent.

Growing up, Judy Martin managed to keep their bills paid on time and afford an annual weeklong trip in the summer to a rented house at Surfside Beach on the Texas Gulf Coast. That getaway always included cousins, aunts, uncles, and a few lucky friends who succeeded in snagging an invite to the annual outing. There was nothing fancy or extravagant about her childhood, but Sam never felt like she was missing out on anything either, and she always knew that her mother and her extended family loved her and were there for her.

As the coffee was brewing, she whipped up her regular breakfast of toast, almond butter, and a banana and then sat quietly at the tiny kitchen table. In the middle of the linoleum topped hand-me-down was a wooden napkin holder, her Grammy's old ladybug salt and pepper shakers, and an old Tupperware container that held pens, sticky notes, paperclips, grocery receipts, some loose change, and a fingernail filer. Detritus that just accumulated after years of life in the small kitchen area. Sam was very tempted to leave one of the sticky notes on the backdoor that said, "The boogeyman can get us if this door isn't locked!"

Sam sighed and shook her head.

Her sweet mother would not be up for a couple more hours. Judy had gotten accustomed to sleeping in since the loss of her accounting job. When the family business she worked for first closed their doors, she made the effort to look for another job, but this had, to date, not led to a new paycheck. Sam would make a note in her planner to discuss home security with her mom, especially since there would be many workers and nosy neighbors visiting the latest bungalow site to bite the dust.

She helped herself to the coffee and sat back down to finish her breakfast. When she was finished eating and the dishes were rinsed and in the drying rack, she crept back to her room, where she quickly put on running shorts and a jog bra. It was not what she wanted to do with her coveted time, but she knew it was the best way to free her mind and think through everything that was pulling on her for attention, both physically and mentally. As she turned to exit her room, she glanced at her latest motivational plaque hanging by her door that read, "If cauliflower can become pizza, you, my friend, can become anything." She kissed her fingertips and touched the frame in a gesture of self-encouragement and thought to herself, *Dear Lord, please let that be true.*

Even though the sun had barely started to peek out behind the live oak trees in the front yard of the house that she shared with her mother, Sam knew that they were in for another scorcher of a day. She was glad that her mom had not awakened before she left, so she had time to think about how to broach the subject again about leaving the house unlocked at night. Not that Sam felt like she was defenseless, she just thought they should do everything they could to watch out for their own safety.

As she moved toward the excavator and the construction workers who were spraying down the debris with water from the old house to control the dust, she looked at some of her neighboring houses with a critical eye. Sam's memories of the houses and neighborhood from her childhood always had fresh paint and front doors with welcoming wreaths and potted plants, tidy front yards, and children that rode around on their bikes until the streetlights came on signaling it was time to head home.

There was the Rutherford's house, which was still owned by the family, and Sam could see that it was almost exactly how she remembered it growing up. The landscaping had been spiffed up and a garage apartment had been tastefully added in the back, but overall, it still had that same cottage charm that endeared so many residents to the GOOF area over the years.

As she walked on and started her warm-up, she examined the other side of the street. Sam couldn't believe that she had not noticed how bad the old Romano house looked. When did the shutters start to droop and lose their slats, and what happened to the window planters that held flowers and were now resting randomly against the house? She knew from personal experience that the homeowner's association had to be filling the new owner's mailbox with violation notifications and warnings.

Sam was starting to work up a sweat as she continued to survey the houses on her regular jogging route. She had to concede that while several older homes were well kept, several cottages truly needed restoration, and she couldn't help but think that these homes had character and style that could be brought back to life with just a little tender loving care.

Hell, who am I fooling? Our house fits in this category, too, and it's going to take more moolah than TLC to get our home back to its former self, Sam snarked to herself.

As she rounded the last corner and was in the home stretch of her workout, she saw one of their longtime neighbors and community watchdog, Mr. Fletcher, out getting his morning paper. Sam smiled and picked up her pace as she ran by his immaculate yard and house and looked straight ahead, so there was no doubt that she was not going to stop and visit. She knew he meant well, but she wasn't up to discussing whatever the latest offense was that the Lamonte Lane home that she loved was committing.

Sam stopped to stretch on the curb in front of their house and took in the whole area with her newfound critical eye. There was no doubt that the cottage was screaming for a new coat of paint, and she knew her mother had started to work on that project if they could scrape the money together to complete the job, but it also needed so much more. She could not recall when the roof and gutters had been updated or cleaned out, and the wooden fence on one side of the house was leaning precariously on some crepe myrtles for support. The flowerbeds in front were mostly weeds, with a few dried-up bushes poking up between the seed heads. She also noted that the mailbox was rusting and was overflowing with catalogs, flyers, magazines, and envelopes.

"Well, I can at least keep us from getting a citation for an unkempt and overflowing mailbox, if there is such a thing," Sam muttered as she pulled what had to be several days' worth of mail out of the box that had lost its lid years ago.

Sam kicked off her tennis shoes and left them at the door as she tried to quietly enter the house while cradling the large stack of unwelcome correspondence. She dumped it all on the couch table where her mom would be sure to see it.

There is no way she can miss this stack that killed a whole tree to create, Sam reasoned. And just as she was about to tiptoe back to their shared bathroom to clean up for her overbooked day, she saw the top envelope from the City of Houston Water Department. It was stamped "Late—Second Notice" on the envelope, and the offending bill showing through the envelope window was on bright yellow paper.

Sam felt her breakfast banana and almond butter start to churn in her stomach and she couldn't tell if her palms were sweating from her recent run or if it was another effect of this upsetting notice. *One more thing to worry about,* she thought to herself as she hurried to get her shower in before her mother woke up, or even worse, before the water was turned off by the city.

"Well, I'll be go to hell again today, and it's not even 8 a.m."

CHAPTER 2

Taking the last corner back to her house as fast as the speed limit and the new mothers walking with their Nuna strollers allowed, Sam made it back to the aging bungalow with only fifteen minutes to freshen up for her late lunch date with her aunt. They were scheduled to meet in Uptown Park, located in the exclusive Houston Galleria area, for a salad.

Sam quickly parked in the tiny circular driveway and let herself in the front door.

"Hey, Mom, it's just me!"

"Sam, I'm coming."

Her mom came around the corner from the bedroom hallway wearing one of her summer muumuus. Normal attire now that she was not going into an office, and she had added a few pounds from being home all the time. Her new fluffier figure wasn't a bad look, it was simply different from the trim build she had had for as long as Sam could remember. The roots from her drugstore enhanced, ash-blonde hair were past due for a touch-up, and she had twisted it up with a claw clip on top of her head. Judy gave her daughter a peck on the cheek and kept right on walking, glancing towards the kitchen table and then towards the small countertop that divided the kitchen and living area.

"What are you looking for, Mom?" Sam asked.

"Um, no big deal, but my cell phone was here just a second ago."

"Okay, remember, I showed you how to ping your cell phone from your watch?"

"No, Sam, I guess I didn't, or I wouldn't still be looking for it," Judy snapped.

"It's okay, let me show you," Sam said as she took her mom's arm and touched the icon on her watch to set off the pinging of the lost phone. Sure enough, there it was, in the kitchen, but hiding under the loaf of bread.

"Here you go, Mom," Sam said, handing Judy her phone. "I need to just rinse off and put on some fresh clothes, and then I'll be leaving."

"What do you have going on? A lunch date with that sweet guy? What's his name again?"

"Mom, you know his name is Leo, but no, just a quick, um, business lunch." Sam sputtered her lie out as convincingly as she could.

Judy Martin looked a little skeptical as she took in this answer and then waved her hands in the air in a shooing motion, indicating to her daughter she had better get going.

Sam made her way into the small bathroom that she shared with her mother, wound her hair on top of her head, and rinsed off in a spitting spray of cool water from the old shower head. When she reemerged from her bedroom, which she had slept in since she was a child, she was decked out in clean leggings, a fresh Barre Babes and Buns T-shirt, a thigh-length wind jacket with the sleeves pushed up, and her cleaner pair of slide-in tennis shoes. The jacket was to hopefully style her look as city chic and not a gym rat on the run.

Passing her mother in the tiny den as she made her way to the kitchen to fill her empty water bottle and gather up her backpack, phone, and keys, she blew a kiss in her direction and reminded her that she had her marketing class later in the evening.

"Oh, yes, that's right. Don't worry about me, Sam. I think I am going to get some more paint samples to test on the house. I'll see you tonight"

Loading everything back in her clunker, Sam felt terrible about not admitting that she was meeting up with Aunt Pookie, her mom's older sister, but Pookie did stress that she wanted to talk to her privately.

Twenty minutes later and only three minutes late, she pulled up to the trendy little health food restaurant that served vegetarian, vegan, or paleo food. Sam did not really care at this point, she was just hungry, bordering on hangry, and anxious to see what this lunch was all about.

She thanked the parking gods that she found a decently close space and ran into the blessedly cool and stylish café. She did not have to look hard to see her beloved aunt waiting in line to order, fanning herself with one of the paper menus. True to nature, she had on a flowing multi-colored kimono over cherry, high-shine stretchy leggings, silver studded tennis shoes, clown-length fake eyelashes, killer white teeth, and her hair moussed up with a lavender bird clipped on the side. If anyone could pull off this look with confidence and aplomb, it was Pookie.

Sam threw her arms around Pookie, gave her a squeeze, and then air-kissed like they were in Paris instead of the Bayou City.

"Helllloooo, darlin', you look precious, as always," Pookie drawled.

"Pookie, I've missed you."

"I know how busy you are, my dear. What with working, school, and keeping an eye on my little sister, I don't know how you have time to have much of a social life. You do remember the theory behind dating and going out, don't you?"

Sam smiled and said, "It's fine. I only have a few more marketing classes left, and I will finally graduate. Then, I can get on with my life."

"How's that cute little tater tot from up north? Please tell me that you make time to share the sugar now and then?"

Sputtering on the last swallow from her water bottle, "You didn't just say that, did you?"

Aunt Pookie was referring to her on-again, off-again relationship with Leo Lavoie. It wasn't that she wasn't interested in the dark-haired, blue-eyed, French Canadian. It was that she could be too interested in him. The carefree, "You Only Live Once" lifestyle that Leo loved to live by had gotten Sam in trouble on several occasions in the past.

They met when Leo's little sister, Brielle, had been visiting him from their home in Huntsville, Ontario. Trying to entertain the then sixteen-year-old teenager, he dropped her off at Bar Babes and Buns for a supervised exercise class while he supposedly finished some work from home. Running late to pick Brielle up when class was over, Sam stayed with the young girl until her dawdling brother came back to retrieve her. Sam had started to let him know what she thought about his tardiness, but when he profusely apologized to both women and offered to take them for a coffee, she could see that he was out of his element trying to be a parental figure to the young girl. The week after Brielle got on the plane to head back to her home in the hilly and wooded area of Muskoka, Leo showed up at the barre studio. This time, Sam agreed to meet him for a drink after work, and she had been charmed ever since. It was hard to do, but Sam had recently decided to pull back from the relationship and try to keep her goals in focus and her mind clear from "sharing the sugar" with Leo.

The two women found an empty table, and a waiter brought their turkey Cobb and avocado Caesar salads to the table.

"So, what did you want to talk to me about, Pook? Not that I don't just love seeing you, but is everything okay?"

"Well, dear, it's about my baby sister."

Sam's head shot up and she looked her aunt in the eye as she asked, "What about her?" Sam immediately thought Pookie must be concerned about her employment status or lack thereof. "Mom's been trying to find another job, but it has just been hard to get a lead on anything right now in the oil and gas industry."

"My dear, you know how much I love you and Judy, and I do hate to be the one to possibly bring this to your attention, but my baby sister seems to be, um, slipping."

Sam just continued staring, and Aunt Pookie thought she wasn't getting her point across. Finally, she sighed and said, "She seems to be so forgetful lately, Sam, and you can't tell me that you haven't noticed that she's not her usual self? Hon, I remember when she was always the quickest and smartest bunny in the forest!"

Sam blinked a few times, and it was like all the puzzle pieces were finally locking into place or a blurry picture was coming into focus. She drifted off for a few seconds and thought to herself about the changes she had seen in her mom recently but had not taken the time from her overloaded schedule to reflect on whether they were normal life changes or something more. Aunt Pookie was the only one brave enough to say it out loud, and that was why she was the leader of the family.

Sam finished chewing and put her fork down. Somewhere in the last several months, Sam had taken over the role as the head of their small household. Sam didn't even know how it happened. Nothing was ever verbally stated, it was just that her mother depended on her more and more for daily tasks, and Sam had been happy to be able to be there for her, but her aunt was right. Something was going on with her sweet mom, and if Sam had to put it into words, she could only say that Judy was experiencing some type of ongoing forgetfulness and lack of follow-through on everyday household jobs and upkeep of the house.

"Look, Sam, I know as well as you do that Judy's memory has been slipping for a while. I realize that she lost her job, and that was no fault of her own, but being home, and socially and intellectually isolated for months just hasn't helped her at all. Also, you know that our family tree does have a bird or two that your Grammy would have said fly a little close to the cuckoo's nest. All genuinely nice birds, but nonetheless, crazy birds. I don't know how else to say that I'm worried about her."

Sam looked at Pookie and nodded her head. "You're right. Mom's been a little forgetful. I promise I'll talk to her and see if she will agree to see her doctor. She's just always been so together and independent that it's hard for me to point it out to her, or to honestly believe that this is happening."

"Aw, honey, if I had my druthers, I'd handle all of this for you, but I know if your mom will listen to anyone, it will be you."

CHAPTER 3

Sam decided that she would go back to the studio, review her school assignment in the back office, teach her four o'clock class, and then head to the University of Houston downtown campus. When Sam had finished high school, she decided to live at home for just a year, take some basics at the community college, and save some money so she could help pay for college. Her original plan to end up at Texas A&M University like her mother somehow never gained any traction. Life happened, and she ended up transferring to the University of Houston, where she was currently trying to finish her bachelor's degree in marketing.

Sam's goal was to try and meet up with her professor about her senior marketing class project that was due in just three short weeks. How did she get so far behind? Normally, she would have the project all researched and written up, with her presentation ready to go well before the due date.

Well, Sam knew what had happened. Worrying about her unemployed mother and the fact that they were not destitute, but as Aunt Pookie would say, they appeared to be low in the hole, had kept her mind preoccupied and unfocused. She had picked up some extra classes to teach to add to the household income, but she could not possibly cover the expenses on her own. Nonetheless, Sam was struggling with how to deal with their financial troubles, and now, days after her lunch with Aunt Pookie, Sam realized that she also needed to be concerned about her mother's ongoing forgetfulness.

When Sam discovered that Judy was late paying the water bill after rescuing the mail from the overstuffed box, she decided that the easiest and most efficient thing for her to do was just to pay it herself. She still planned on talking to Judy about the household finances, but at the time, that was just the quickest way to make sure that they continued to have running water. This also gave Sam more time to figure out the best way to bring up the sensitive topic.

Judy had always paid the utility bills and managed the house finances and upkeep. Sam had taken over all her personal bills and paid for as much of her tuition as she could when she first started her higher education journey and basics at Houston Community College. That was years ago, and she felt more than a little bit guilty that she had never offered to do more financially to support the household. Not that she could do that much, but she would have thought of something to help moneywise if she had known that her mom was struggling to make ends meet. Sam had always assumed the severance package that Judy received when her job ended was enough to live on until she found another position somewhere.

It was just such a surprise. The late notice that almost made her lose her breakfast was the wake-up call that Sam needed to look a little further into their household's financial standing.

Sam had thought her mom probably received online bill payment notices for all her utilities, mortgage, and credit cards like most people today, but she honestly had not paid much attention because everything just always *worked*. The water came on when she showered, the lights came on when she flipped the switch, and the little sanctuary that they called their home on Lamonte Lane was always just a given.

After her unplanned run from earlier in the week, she had carefully gone through all the mail that she brought in that morning, including the pile that she found on the messy desk in Judy's tiny home office, another unusual thing. Judy had always been meticulously neat. During Sam's snoop session, she found three other notifications, including one from GOMO, or the Golden Oaks Maintenance Organization. That particular piece of correspondence said the annual homeowner's association fee was now eight months late. It also stated that the peeling paint on the house was past due to be refurbished and was now out of compliance with the maintenance organization's regulations, and they would be turning over the entire matter to their legal counsel if the situation was not rectified promptly.

Now it made sense why her mom had been working on new paint selections, and Sam was glad that Judy had taken the GOMO notice seriously. Sam still needed to talk to her about the late HOA fee, but her attention to the paint situation was a positive step.

Sam was definitely in worry mode now that Aunt Pookie had pointed out how Judy seemed to be slowly drifting further and further away from the smart, independent woman that she had always been. She was going to have to be a real adult and also confront her mother about her mental cloudiness as well as their arrival into the lower of the lower class. *Who said being an adult was fun?* she smirked.

After straightening and cleaning up the studio after her last class, Sam got in her 2010 Jeep Cherokee. She swore she was going to drive the vehicle until the wheels fell off, and with 179,000 miles on old Booger, Sam thought that she was probably going to get her wish. The air conditioner worked, which is a huge plus in Texas, but there were not any other bells and whistles on the clunker. The cloth seats were grungy, to say the least, and the hand-cranked tinted windows were starting to bubble and peel from the heat. The original owner had kept up with the oil changes and tire rotations, so Sam felt like she did have that in her favor, but the color was such an awful shade of murky, drab green, that no one would ever really think it was a cool vehicle. Sam had gotten it at a fair price and was consoled by reminding herself that she had saved enough money when she bought the Booger to pay for one of her college classes along with some new leggings and workout tops for work.

Traffic in Houston is always unpredictable, but it is either bad, really bad, or pack some survival gear bad. Sam jumped on I-45 South and headed towards the downtown campus of the University of Houston. Praying for the best but prepared for the worst, Sam made the commute after only a thirty-minute jaunt as she pulled into the Vine Street Garage adjacent to the school of business.

Gathering her backpack, cellphone, and car keys, she was about to open the Booger's door when she noticed that another car was pulling in right next to her. If Sam thought the Booger was hard to miss with its ugly paint job and pimply window tinting, the bright red Audi sports coupe was just as noticeable, and it belonged to Nic.

Nic Tello was not on Sam's favorite person list right now. The smooth-talking flirt was always looking for his next conquest, and Sam did not like the way Nic was leading Darby, one of the barre tenders at work, on like she might have a chance at becoming his next shiny toy. Sam knew his type. He had one eye on Darby when they were together, and his other eye was always scanning the area for his next dalliance.

Nic locked his car with a remote that tweeted and flashed the headlights, indicating it was secure, and waited for Sam to gather her gear and lock the Booger. Not that anyone would ever find the beater worth breaking into, it was a habit and Sam thought it good practice for when she could afford a shiny, cool vehicle with automatic windows that were acne-free.

"Hey, Sam, how's it going?"

"It's fine, but I'm sorry I can't talk right now. I'm trying to see my professor during her office hours, and by my calculations, I only have twenty minutes left."

"No worries. I'm meeting up with my team members for a gaming development class."

Nic was *not* good boyfriend material, but he *was* a computer whiz. Nic's family had money from grandparents and great-grandparents who were smart enough to buy commercial real estate in Houston and the surrounding area before Houston grew into the fourth largest city in the United States. They had originally wanted Nic to embrace his heritage and go to work at the family business that oversaw everything from the development and leasing of new properties to new construction management of the family real estate. Nic, however, was used to getting his own way and doing what Nic wanted to do. What was supposed to be a gap year in Europe, eventually turned into two years, and left him uncommitted to anything until he enrolled in the computer science program at the University of Houston. Much to the displeasure of his family, Nic was happily taking just enough hours each semester to be considered a full-time student and a part-time party animal. With tuition paid for each semester, a nice condo off Washington Avenue, full membership to the Houstonian Country Club, and an American Express black card that had no limits, Nic certainly appeared to live a charmed life.

They walked in silence for a few seconds towards the campus, and Sam heard him inhale, "Look, I know what you think about me, but I honestly think Darby is great. She just doesn't trust me. Would you please tell her to give me a chance and go out with me?"

Sam cut her eyes and said, "Seriously? Every time I see you, which isn't that often, you're all cozy with the flavor of the day. I don't want to see you lead her on for a week or two and then have to console her when she is heartbroken over you."

Darby was more than just a co-worker; she was a good friend. They had both recognized their kindred spirits when she came into the studio to interview for the front desk job. Darby was positive and enthusiastic during the interview, and a recent move from Cullman, Alabama, made her eager to find some stable income. Sam and the studio owner, Cara Womack, hired her on the spot. She made a terrific addition to the atmosphere of the studio, and Sam soon discovered that Darby was also trying to finish college while she leased a garage apartment with two other roommates. Tight quarters for sure, but economically and logistically more secure.

They had met Nic on a rare night out when the girls had gone to have a quick drink at one of the downtown bars. Hoping to sit in a quiet corner on an inner-city Houston rooftop and enjoy the sunset, they quickly realized that so many others had the same idea. Rounding the corner, they saw that Nic and a group of his friends had taken up most of the seating area. Although the sun had not gone all the way down, the crew was well on their way to an inebriated evening. As Sam was about to turn and lead Darby back the way they came from, Nic spotted the petite brunette and the statuesque blonde pair and asked them to join the rest of his gang. That meeting was over three months ago.

"I promise, I'm sincerely interested in getting to know Darby. I just need your help convincing her that I'm not playing games."

Opening the door to the building, Sam turned to him and said, "I'm not sure that *I'm* convinced, and I don't have enough time to discuss it with you. The next time I see her, I will suggest she give a *real* date with you a try. However, if I hear that one scuzzy thing comes out of your mouth or you so much as try and pretend you are a player, or whatever the latest terminology is, I'll personally track you down."

"You will?"

Sam's mouth opened to elaborate on what she would do to him if he led Darby on when he hastily added, "I mean not to track me down, but that you will talk to her. I promise I will treat Darby like a princess."

Sam silently shook her head and made a mental note to reach out to Darby as she continued walking down the hall to meet with Professor Wood. Nic decided he would take their conversation as a win and left Sam as she power-walked towards her teacher's office.

Sam knocked on the office door and then waited until she heard her professor invite her to enter the small work-room. Professor Chrisha Wood was not what you would describe as your typical tenured teacher. In the same age group as Sam's mother, her small office was neatly and tastefully decorated with a plastic reusable pan full of fresh, homemade cookies on the credenza, along with framed pictures of all her children and grandchildren.

"Hello, Ms. Martin, please come in and sit down. I looked over the proposal for your project, and I have to say that it is light on research and substance and full of, um, fluff."

"Professor Wood, I know, and I assure you, I am planning on adding to my project. I was just hoping that you could give me some direction. I'm having a little trouble with the focal point of my proposal. Is there an objective or target that you think I should focus on?"

Professor Wood leaned back in her chair, popped the top off the plastic container of her latest batch of cookies, and removed a bite-sized treat for herself. "Well, let's start with this, what is something that interests and motivates *you*?"

Sam didn't hesitate to answer, "I always thought I would work this project into the necessities and complexities of opening a boutique fitness studio."

"I'm sure that could work, even though it has been done many times, if that is a subject matter that truly motivates you. Here, Ms. Martin, try my latest oatmeal raisin cookie recipe, and we can discuss this further."

CHAPTER 4

When Sam was getting back into her car, she felt her phone vibrating in her backpack. She grabbed the phone as she unloaded everything into her backseat and saw that she had missed a phone call from her mom, and she had three text messages from Darby. The first message from Darby told Sam that the studio was cleaned and locked up. The next message was asking Sam how her meeting went with Professor Wood, and the final message was asking if Sam wanted to join her in eating some Blue Bell Pecan Pralines 'n Cream ice cream to help give herself a brain freeze and hopefully forget her boyfriend troubles.

Sam decided that if she could listen to Darby vent about Nic and feast on ice cream while she was being a good friend, it would be a win-win. Maybe Sam could also use this opportunity to encourage Darby to go on a real date with Nic and not just run into him at some of the local hangouts.

Sam started the car, sent Darby a text that she was on her way to her Height's area garage apartment and to have a spoon ready, and then called her mom on speaker phone.

Judy answered the phone on the first ring and said, "Hi, Sam."

"Hi, Mom, I saw I missed your call."

"Do you know when you are going to be home? That crotchety old coot, Mr. Fletcher, wants me to turn in the paperwork to sign up for the Neighborhood Watch program. I just can't tell him that I need another form. He's already brought me two, and he said he is not going to help me with my new house paint approval with the homeowner's association until I return that form."

Edwin Fletcher always looked like he was getting ready to plow the back forty in his blue jean overalls and his neatly pressed plaid shirt. The sides of the overalls were never buttoned, and Sam was always afraid to look or ask if that was for ventilation of some sort or if they were just uncomfortable. Edwin was a retired veteran who now made it his full-time job to keep the GOOF area in tip-top shape. He was an officer on the homeowner's association board, but he went well beyond the normal call of duty. He knew who was out of town, who had overnight guests, and who needed help to bring their home up to the homeowner's association standards, even if that help was not requested.

"I'm going by Darby's for a quick visit. Then I'll be home, and we can look for the form and get it turned in to Mr. Fletcher. Don't worry, Mom, we'll find it."

By the time Sam pulled up to Darby's apartment, she was ready for her own pint of ice cream. How was she going to find the time to get the additional research needed for her marketing project, talk to her mom about seeing a doctor and the past due bills, and get the house paint up to code? *Sheesh*, she thought, *Do I get some other instructors to cover my classes so I can work on some of these things, or do I ask them if I can take any of their scheduled classes to help with our money situation?*

As Sam got out of the Booger, she decided that she would look at her ever-present planner when she got home and get everything planned out and scheduled to help her feel more in control of her life, which was currently careening out of control. Sam's security blanket was her glittery, turquoise-colored day planner that said, "Hold on, let me overthink this!" on the cover. She realized that as a millennial, she should be opposed to her old-fashioned, tab-sectioned day planner, but she always felt more in control of her life with the calendar organizer literally at her fingertips. She got teased by everyone who really knew her that the planner was her constant companion and a substitute for what should be a loving pet or partner.

Darby greeted her at the top of the stairs to the garage apartment in an oversized sweatshirt that hung to her mid-thigh and with two spoons in her hand. She wore her straight dark hair at chin level that she kept tucked behind her ears, and at five feet two inches tall, and with her clear, makeup-less face, she could easily be mistaken for a teenager.

Sam gave her a hug, grabbed the spoon, and said, "Spill."

"Oh, girl, I am so embarrassed. I saw Nic last night at Saint Arnold Brewery with just a couple of his computer gaming friends. I thought, surely I can hold his attention without any of his normal sleaze bucket groupies around."

"Sounds reasonable."

"All I said was, 'Y'all must be worn slap out of talking about video games,' and the entire table of losers burst out laughing. My Alabama twang and terminology make me look and feel like I'm an idiot," Darby said with a wobbling voice and watery eyes.

"Darby, your accent, and Alabama phrases are part of what make you so irresistibly cute—and *you*. Next time you see them you just need to start with one of your 'Bless your heart' phrases and end it with 'but why are you all such assholes?' That means you're still being sweet, right?"

Darby's lips started to curve into a slight smile. "Honestly, Nic didn't say anything, and I practically ran back to my table of friends, where I'm afraid I was over-served. With the alcohol flowing, I may have decided that I could dance really good . . . by myself . . . close to their table . . . until I knocked a chair over."

Sam grabbed the ice cream container and shoveled another bite onto her spoon. "Well, maybe the next time he asks you out, you should give him the chance for some one-on-one time. Maybe if Nic doesn't have a party going on around him, you two can have a real conversation and get to know each other."

"Well, if the good Lord's willing and the creek doesn't rise, I may give him a chance."

Sam smiled and said, "That's my Alabama girl."

CHAPTER 5

As Sam pulled onto her street after her ice cream session with Darby, she could see every window of their home lit up and shining brightly. She parked, gathered an armful of the day's remnants, and walked through the back door. She was not surprised to hear Aerosmith playing throughout the house, and her mom belting out a song about walking the right way along with Steven Tyler.

"Mom? What are you doing?"

When she didn't get an answer, Sam walked around to the small office, and she found Judy in the same muumuu she left her in that morning. Standing with her back to her daughter and swaying and singing as she finished emptying the old metal file cabinet of its file folders and paperwork, Sam asked her again, "Sooo, what are we doing now?"

Judy didn't miss a beat as she turned to Sam and said, "I've been as busy as a moth in a mitten since I talked to you. I'm going to get rid of some of this old paperwork that I don't need anymore, and maybe I'll be able to find things more easily when I need them. I even found the Neighborhood Watch form that I need to turn in to Mr. Grumpy-Ass. Hon, help me take these bags to the recycle bin outside."

Sam looked down at the two stuffed garbage bags full of

old bills, mail, magazines, and newspapers. "Are you sure that all this stuff is garbage? Should we go through it together before it's hauled to the city dump or recycled, and it's gone forever?"

Judy cut her eyes to Sam and said, "I went through every bit of this as I was cleaning. I assure you, I am only clearing out what is not necessary, trash or junk. Look, I even made new folders for all my current statements and bank information. I'm going to get caught up on all my bills now. I was simply confused about which ones I needed to pay."

Sam looked inside the old filing cabinet, and sure enough, inside were neatly labeled files that had titles such as "Utilities" and "National Bank of Texas", which was the mortgage holder on the Golden Oaks cottage.

Well, only the state of Texas would think they deserved to have their own national bank, Sam mused to herself.

Taking a deep breath and thinking this was the perfect organic segue, Sam continued, "You know, Mom, now that you mention it, I saw that you had a late notice for the water bill that I was more than happy to take care of. I also saw that GOMO sent you a statement that you are late on the annual fee and the house needs a new paint job. Why didn't you tell me that you were having trouble with the bills? I want to help."

Judy stopped swaying to the music and said, "It's all fine, dear. I admit that I have been a little distracted lately, and I decided that I just needed to get organized. Now that I have everything labeled and in a folder, I can figure out what bills need my attention. You need to stop worrying about me and just concentrate on getting that degree and opening your own health club. And as for the homeowner's association, you know I have already started working on new paint selections for the house."

Once Sam had gotten certified and started teaching classes for Barre Babes and Buns, she knew that what she truly wanted to do was open her own studio. Her business blueprint, which she had only in her mind, incorporated exercise classes along with some retail space and maybe even offer some classes on nutrition and personal well-being. This dream encouraged her to get her marketing degree and continue to teach exercise classes while saving what little money she could to get started in her studio. It was also one of the reasons that her current marketing class project was so important to her and she thought could become the business plan she had been trying to assimilate. If things went well, she could open more studios or franchise her strategy to other fitness enthusiasts. But first things first.

"So, speaking of distractions, I *have* noticed that you have trouble finding some items, and you seem a little confused when we are talking about some things. You know, maybe we can make an appointment to have you checked out by Dr. Chen. Just some basic blood work and a good physical. I'll be happy to take you."

Judy eyed her daughter and said, "I'll think about it, but I can take myself. I'm not helpless, you know. Now go on and work on your school project. I'm going to finish up in here and call it a day."

As Sam walked out of the study after her long day, she was happy to hear that Judy was still singing and had moved on to Boston's *More than a Feeling*. Sam wasn't sure if she was *feeling* like her mom had taken her seriously about the doctor's visit, but she would add it to her to-do list.

CHAPTER 6

Sam woke up later than usual the next morning since she wasn't scheduled for an early morning class and had stayed up rather late reorganizing her schedule and working on her marketing project. Feeling rather pleased with herself, she wandered into the kitchen to make a cup of coffee and to start her toast, almond butter, and banana breakfast routine. She was a creature of habit when it came to her day planner and her breakfast.

It took Sam a moment to realize that the house was too quiet. Her mom always had the television tuned to the morning news show. A quick glance in the sink, and there was Judy's empty cereal bowl.

Sam backtracked to her mom's bedroom and the study only to find her bed made and the study looking better than it had in ages. She slipped on her Birkenstock knock-offs and opened the door to the backyard, where she found Judy. She had spread out an old painter's drop cloth next to the backside of the house and was in the process of mixing and stirring the new sample color paints that she had bought from the local hardware store. Wearing another seasoned muumuu and her hair tied back with a faded blue bandana, she was preparing to paint sample areas on the back of the house to get an idea of how she liked the colors.

Well, this is going to be a problem, Sam thought to herself.

The colors that Judy was preparing to test paint were blindingly bright.

"What are the new colors you are testing today, Mom?" Sam asked as she squinted her eyes at the other failed test spots.

"I picked up this beautiful Clementine and Berry Spice. I'm not sure if I can have an orange-hued home though, I am still a Texas Aggie at heart. Anyway, you know that burnt orange tone is just not in my color wheel, so this one is probably a waste of time."

Well, that is not burnt orange, Mom, like the University of Texas color, that's, um, really . . . vibrant . . . orange, like a traffic cone."

"I'm just trying to give our tiny home a facelift. All these new houses around here have fancy brick and stonework with new landscaping. One of these colors is going to give this old girl the attention she deserves, and maybe she won't look like she's been hit with the ugly stick."

The Golden Oaks and Oak Forest neighborhoods were an area of town that her mom had selected to live in years ago because she could afford the mortgage on her single income and had reasonably good public schools while Sam was growing up. Now that the area had turned into the cool place to be, millennials and investors were buying up the old houses and tearing them down to put up their McMansions as fast as they could schedule the construction crews.

The newly built, huge, two-story homes pushed the limits of the property easements until the houses looked like they were built on postage stamp-sized lots. Sam thought the new houses by and large looked out of place, but these homes were why Judy now felt their little bungalow needed a makeover.

"These colors are not going to be approved by the homeowner's association because they are too, um, intense. Mr. Fletcher talked to you about the guidelines, and the colors are supposed to be 'naturally occurring in nature and generally neutral,'" Sam said, making air quotes. "And another thing, Mom, even a new coat of paint isn't going to cover up the fact that the house needs a new roof and the rotting boards around the windows need replacing. Heck, the windows need replacing, too, for that matter."

Judy picked up a fresh brush to start the next sample can. "That's exactly why I chose these two new colors! Clementines and berries occur in nature." She dipped her brush into the sample can and then added, "I can only work on one project at a time, and as for Mr. Fletcher, he could make a preacher cuss."

CHAPTER 7

Gathering her day's worth of gear, Sam loaded the Booger and headed to the studio to prepare for her first class of the day. Because she wasn't slated until the 10 a.m. morning class, she planned to review her schedule for the rest of the week and reach out to Dr. Chen's office to arrange a general physical for her mom.

As Sam turned onto the studio's street and approached the strip center, she could see that the parking lot was full of cars from the current class that was in session, including a familiar late-model, two-door silver Toyota Solara. Sam knew that this car belonged to a class regular, Dolly Bunosky, who never failed to amuse and impress her with some of the ensembles that she pulled together.

Pulling into the alley behind the storefront where the business owners and workers were supposed to park, Sam unloaded the Booger and was walking towards the front entrance when she did a double take. Leaning against the frame of the door and perusing his cell phone, was Leo.

Leo Lavoie was one of the newest associates at McKinney and Alba, one of the largest law firms in the Houston area. His goal was to work for a firm that specialized in international finance and eventually use his finance and law degree to travel and see the world. One of the middle children in a close-knit family of eight siblings, Leo was determined to expand his horizons beyond the protective bubble he was raised in growing up in the Canadian wilderness. That was one of several reasons he decided to come to the diverse city of Houston to pursue his higher education and law degree. Sam always thought that the main reason had to be to get to a climate where he could show off his beautiful body that was not concealed by items such as parkas, gloves, and hats.

Sam licked her lips to try and disguise not putting on actual lip gloss, and she automatically stood up straighter and sucked in her already tight abs. "Hi, Leo. Are you ready to see if you can make it through one of my barre classes?"

Leo kicked himself upright from the glass door that he was leaning on and reached out to take Sam's backpack, lunch bag, and keys so that all she was left with was her liter reusable water bottle. Sam thought to herself, *Not only are you good-looking, but you have the manners of a true Southern gentleman. I could definitely be convinced to share some sugar with you.*

"Hello, ma belle, I was hoping if I saw you in person you wouldn't be able to turn me down for dinner tonight."

Sam led him into the studio, feeling his gaze on her backside as she walked to the office. *Lord, thank you for guiding me to wear my unsnagged, clean leggings and a matching pair of socks, even if you didn't direct me to put on any makeup.*

"I would love to have dinner, Leo, but can we plan it for another night? I have a marketing class project that I have got to devote some time to, and I am trying to be at home a little more to help Mom around the house."

"Bring her with you. How is mon amie, Judy? Is her new flowerbed holding up in this heat?

The last time Leo had seen Judy, he had stopped by the house to see if he could catch Sam at home but had ended up being recruited into moving landscape pavers from the trunk of Judy's car to the backyard to frame the area around her treasured fruit trees. A job that ended up costing Sam a back rub to rid him of his sore muscles and some sugar sharing to make Sam feel better in general. And this was a prime example of how distracting Leo could be in her life.

"I tell you what, why don't we meet up at the beginning of next week? That will give me a chance to put a little brain time into my project, help Mom with her latest chore, and then you can catch me up on the recent happenings of the Lavoie clan."

Sam didn't feel like she should mention that she was worried about her mom paying the bills and that she was concerned that the GOOF neighborhood was going to be none too pleased with Judy's latest painting efforts. She also didn't want to go into detail about her mom's memory fog that seemed to be getting thicker with each passing day.

Leo leaned forward and emptied his hands of all her personal articles onto the counter, and then smoothly moved even closer to place a warm, gentle kiss on Sam's lips. Sam leaned into the sweetness until she remembered her questionable coffee and almond butter breath and pulled back with a grin. "You know I'm onto your moves now, right?"

"As long as they still work, I'm going to keep on using them. I'll see you soon, belle âme."

Sam started to unload her bag and thought to herself that she was going to have a tough time not sharing any sugar with a man who looked like that and could say such sweet things with such a sexy accent. Aunt Pookie would be proud.

While Sam was waiting for the 9 a.m. class to wind down, she was happy that she was able to schedule an appointment for her mom with Dr. Chen for the next day for a basic physical. She made a note in her day planner to get someone to cover one of her classes just in case the appointment ran late. After checking the appointment off her to-do list and adding the details of the appointment to her organizer, she moved on to doing some research and working on her marketing assignment.

Making some headway on the background information and data that she needed for her project, she was surprised that time had passed so quickly, and she could hear the cool-down music starting that was signaling the end of the class. She left the office and went out front to greet the clients who were leaving and to see if she could help at the front desk.

Ms. Bunosky, a retired public school teacher, was leading the way out of the studio wearing a neon green leggings and shirt combo that made her look like she was trying to imitate a highlighter. The tank top said "Barre Hoppin", and she had a matching armful of plastic bracelets. Sam thought you had to give her an A for effort for showing up to class regularly and an A+ for her entertaining attire.

"Sam, I am so glad I got to see you this morning. Edwin and I were talking last night, and he told me that your mom may need some help with paint selections for y'all's home."

Ms. Bunosky had lived in the GOOF area longer than Sam and her mother and was plugged into the neighborhood gossip arena and chatter. Sam wasn't surprised that Dolly had talked to Edwin, but she hoped that Mr. Fletcher wasn't sharing the fact that the house was in trouble with the maintenance organization and behind on the homeowner's dues. The front of the house, with its peeling paint, looked pretty bad, and everyone who drove by could clearly see its imperfections. It wouldn't take much to conclude that the strict HOA would be stepping in to make sure the house didn't drag the rest of the neighborhood down.

Sam chuckled and tried to distract Ms. Bunosky from the real issue and said, "You know Mr. Fletcher, he's worried about every little thing happening in the neighborhood."

Ms. Bunosky tilted her artificially flaming-red head, squinted her vivid, blue-lined eyelids, and announced loudly enough to turn the heads of several ladies leaving the studio, "Edwin is a caring and generous soul, Sam. I would think you would appreciate the help he is offering your mom?"

Lowering her voice and trying to divert attention away from their conversation, Sam said, "Oh, no, I'm not saying that his help isn't welcome, it's just that I know my mom would die if she thought she was the talk of the neighborhood."

"Sam, you can see that I have an artistic flair and a knack for picking out the correct shade for clothes, makeup, and hair. Why don't you let me come by and help Judy make a suitable selection for the house paint?"

Sam was hoping that her jaw did not remain hanging open too long before she smiled sweetly and told her how nice it would be to have her *artistic* input. As Sam watched Ms. Bunosky walk to her car with a bumper sticker that said, "Too Glam to Give a Damn", she wasn't sure that glow-in-the-dark Dolly was the right person to help Judy with color choices that would meet with the homeowner association's approval—but it was certainly nice of her to offer.

CHAPTER 8

The following day, Sam thought her mom was moving slowly on purpose, but she pretended not to notice as she stood at the front door holding Judy's purse, house keys, and her water bottle.

"Mom, this is not a big deal. We are just going to let Dr. Chen give you a physical and make sure everything is working as it should be. Easy-peasy. We are lucky that she had a cancellation when I called, and she can see you so quickly. Now, please get in the car, or we're going to be late."

Judy came out of her room in one of her signature muumuus and flip-flops and walked past Sam without saying a word.

Sam sighed and loaded all their things into the Booger. She flipped on the radio, tuned it to a seventies station, and headed out of the neighborhood. Before she had even made it to the 610 Loop, she noticed that her mom was singing softly along with Glen Campbell. How could her mother remember the words to all the seventies and eighties classic rock and country songs that she had ever heard, but couldn't remember to pay the bills or where her phone was?

Sam scored a front-row bingo parking spot and ushered her mom into the doctor's office. Judy checked in at the reception desk and was given a clipboard that had several pages to update and fill out for her appointment.

Flipping slowly through the pages, Judy whispered, "Do they really need all this information? I thought this was just a simple checkup."

"It's just standard paperwork, Mom. Just fill it out so we can get you to the back to see the doctor."

Sam pulled her phone from her backpack and was busy scanning her email when she glanced over at Judy, who was dawdling and filling out the questionnaire with a frown on her face. "What's the matter?"

"Nothing. This is good enough," and she walked to the front desk and turned the paperwork into the receptionist.

Just as Judy started to sit back down, the nurse, Cathy, opened the door to the exam room and called her name.

"Wait!"

Everyone was startled and turned to see the receptionist with her clipboard and the unfinished paperwork that had just been turned in. "Ms. Martin, you skipped a few pages, and you didn't sign these forms or initial where I had marked for you!"

Cathy had been Dr. Chen's nurse since they started seeing her, and always kept the office running smoothly. She took the forms from the receptionist and said, "I've got this. We can finish while I get her set up in an exam room."

Catching Cathy's eye, Sam mouthed a thank you. When she made the appointment for her mom, she was able to relay her concerns and the purpose of the visit so that Judy couldn't dismiss the real reason that she was seeing the doctor once they were there in person.

Sam settled back into her chair and continued to check

her messages and her to-do list in her daily planner. She blocked off a night the following week for dinner with Leo and added the classes she agreed to take for the instructor who switched with her so that she could be at today's appointment with her mom. Sam also made a note to call Aunt Pookie and let her know that she had succeeded in getting her mom to the doctor's office and how today's visit went.

After twenty minutes, the door opened, and Cathy said, "Sawyer, Dr. Chen would like you to join her in her office with your mom."

Sam was startled to hear her name, stood, and walked towards the door. "Is everything okay?"

"I'm sure it's all fine. Dr. Chen just thinks it's always better to have an extra set of ears during these discussions."

In her early forties, Dr. Haylee Chen was personable and kind, and Sam had started seeing her when she was a teenager and needed physicals to play sports. Sam had always thought the good doctor looked like she should be on a fashion runway with her stylish clothes, and she envied how pulled together and classy she always looked. She had continued to see her for everything from sore throats to flu shots, and Judy had become a regular patient when she had some blood work done and found that she had high cholesterol.

Dr. Chen was wearing a traditional white lab coat over her Chloe Dao high-waisted plaid pencil skirt with a light-blue linen ruffled top and Valentino studded sneakers. Her straight black hair was pulled back into a low ponytail, and she had on tasteful gold hoop earrings and a small wedding band on her hands that were neatly and professionally manicured.

When Sam walked into the back office, her mom was already sitting in one of the guest chairs, and Dr. Chen signaled for Sam to take the empty chair as she gracefully settled herself in place behind her desk.

"Sam, it's good to see you. You look as fit as ever. I know I keep saying it, but I'm going to make it to one of your classes soon."

Sam smiled to herself. Dr. Chen had been saying that for years. She couldn't rule out seeing her at the studio one day, but Sam knew that when she wasn't busy at her practice, she was an involved mom who had two elementary school-aged children at home. There were pictures of the two little girls with long black hair and designer matching outfits in a silver frame on her desk.

"So, let's talk. I understand that there are some concerns about Judy's memory and some general forgetfulness. Let me start by telling you both that some memory-related issues are normal as we age and can happen to all of us. For example, forgetting someone's name or being temporarily confused about the day of the week. We might also struggle to find the right word or misplace an item. These are all normal things that happen because, as our body changes over time, so does our brain. However, memory issues can be attributed to other things such as sleep deprivation, stress, side effects of medication, or even dehydration. The best thing to do right now is run some tests, and let's rule out some of these things to see what we are truly dealing with. I want to let you both know that if we do rule out some medical issues that may be causing your memory issues, Judy, I will refer you to a neurologist for further evaluation."

"Dr. Chen, did Mom mention to you that she had an aunt and a grandfather who possibly had some type of memory problem? Is this something that could be hereditary?" Sam slid her eyes toward her mom to see how she was taking all this information. Her lips were pinched, and she noticed that Judy glanced longingly at her purse, where Sam knew she kept her natural anxiety supplements and emergency smokes.

Her mom never really smoked, but on occasion, she was known to enjoy a cigarillo with a Tito's and sparkling water. Lavender and chamomile was suggested when she first lost her job in the oil market downturn, and she was stressed about finding new employment, but overall, she led a pretty clean life. Or a boring one.

Dr. Chen waited to answer her until she made direct eye contact with Sam and then said, "Good question. Most dementia is not passed down to children and grandchildren, but there are rare types that do have a strong genetic link or that may make you more susceptible to developing dementia."

Sam knew that her longtime physician was trying to relieve her own mind, and Sam said a silent prayer as she bit her lip so that she didn't shout out loud, "Thank you, baby Jesus!"

"Judy, I'm going to get you set up for some lab work, an EEG, and an MRI of the brain. All painless procedures, but this will help to point us in the direction that we need to go next. Any questions?"

Sam and Judy both shook their heads no, said their goodbyes, and then they were shepherded to the checkout area, where nurse Cathy had all the paperwork ready for the upcoming tests. Handing Judy the forms, she said,

"When we get all the results back, we will call you and schedule a follow-up appointment."

As they got back in the Booger, Sam noticed that her mom had immediately covered her eyes with her sunglasses and was noticeably quiet.

"Mom, I have a couple of hours before I have to be back at the studio, why don't we go have an early dinner?"

She had blocked out the next couple of hours for work on her marketing project, but this situation qualified for a change in Sam's rigid schedule.

"No, I think I would just like to go home, but thank you."

"It's all going to be fine. You heard what Dr. Chen said, your memory . . . uh, the problem could be caused by several things. Let's not get upset until we know what we are really dealing with."

When Sam pulled up to the house to drop Judy off, her mom mumbled just loud enough to be heard and said, "I'm going to rule out dehydration with my friend, Mr. Tito."

Sam smirked and told her to be careful, stay home if she was visiting with Tito, and that she would be home later that night when she got off work.

CHAPTER 9

Going through her mental checklist of things to do, Sam called Aunt Pookie on the way back to work to go over everything that Dr. Chen had discussed with them. When she didn't answer the call, Sam left her a brief message and told her to call her back when she had a chance to talk about the appointment. Sam was also hoping that she could recruit Pookie to take her sister for some of the tests that were scheduled when they left the doctor's office.

She felt the need to discuss her mom's doctor's visit with her aunt and realized again how important she was in her life. Her mother had three sisters, all of whom were born and raised in Texas, but Aunt Pookie was the oldest of the four siblings and the favorite aunt of all her cousins. How could she not be? Pookie never had children of her own, so she was the go-to family person for anything that your mom, dad, grandparents, or other aunts did not have the time or energy to handle. As the reigning matriarch of the family, Pookie was in the know and available to help at a moment's notice when family business needed to be handled or you needed help. Sam needed help.

Instead of going all the way back to the University of Houston campus to work on her assignment, Sam decided to save the time and headache of driving there and work in the back office of the barre studio. If she was lucky, she could sneak inside during class, and she wouldn't be side-tracked by some of the clients who liked to visit at the end of each session.

When Sam was all set up in front of her laptop with her notes and rough draft in place to start on her latest changes to her report, her mind started to drift. She thought to herself, *I'll just do a quick search online and try to understand a little bit more about what Mom and I might be facing with her memory issue.*

Thirty minutes later, Sam sat back and closed her eyes. She had thought that she was going to make herself feel better about researching some of the basics, but what she found on her information quest was overwhelming. The first thing that she learned was that dementia, which included Alzheimer's, and was the most common form of dementia, was devastating to the individual as well as to their loved ones. She learned that in America alone, millions of people were living with Alzheimer's, and the number was rising every year with the aging population. She also discovered that one in three seniors dies with some form of dementia and that the costs to care for and treat these patients could literally break a family. *At the rate we are going, it won't take much to break us,* Sam thought.

Making some notes so that she could be sure and follow up with Dr. Chen, Sam forced herself to focus on the real reason she was locked in the back office of the studio, her marketing project.

Sam finally got herself on track and was so focused that she jumped when she heard Darby knock on the office door and say, "Girlfriend, I know you are hiding in here, but I'm locking up the studio for the night."

Sam stood and opened the door, and she saw that Darby hardly looked like she had been working. In fact, she looked fashionable in a little black romper with strappy, platform shoes. She had dusted her cheeks with some color, and her lips were bright pink instead of glistening with sweat and no makeup at all.

Sam smiled and asked, "You're not doing anything special tonight, right? Maybe going home to do your laundry and maybe watch a little TV?"

Darby beamed as she did a little twirl. "What do you think? Classy and yet still a little sexy?"

"You look perfect. Where is Nic taking you, and please don't tell me to one of his regular hangouts with his gaming groupies?"

"He's meeting me at Brenner's on the Bayou for dinner. I told him I had to work late, and I feel better having my own ride in case I decide he's had his last chance with me."

Brenner's was a Houston institution that had been in business since the 1930s. Not in its original setting, but now located off the ever-classy Memorial Drive, the restaurant enjoys the space to showcase a picturesque garden with water features and a gazebo. It could be quite romantic, and Sam thought it was a good place for Darby to get to know Nic without being interrupted by a group that wanted to play beer pong, flip cup, or quarters.

"Text me afterward and just give me a thumbs up or a thumbs down. I'll be able to read between the lines."

Sam told Darby to lock the door behind her and that she would finish shutting everything down when she was ready to go home. She sent a quick text to her mom letting her know that she was going to stay at the quiet studio for another hour or so and work on her project in the peace and quiet. As Sam tried to focus on the work at hand, her mind continually returned to her mother's memory issues and the few surprising facts that she had learned earlier about dementia. The more she chewed on the situation, the more she realized that there had to be something that she could do to help. Not only her mother, but other families that found themselves in similar situations.

Deciding that she wasn't making any more progress on her schoolwork and that she couldn't stop thinking about her mother, Sam decided they both needed a pick-me-up. Locking the studio and loading her things in the passenger seat of the Booger, she headed towards Rosie's Pizzeria to get a vegetarian pizza to-go for them to share and a bottle of wine for herself at the neighborhood liquor store. She knew that if her mom had been visiting with Mr. Tito this afternoon, the food would do her good.

CHAPTER 10

For the next couple of days, Sam worked on her assignment between her scheduled times at Barre Babes and Buns and showed up at campus early to put in some more research before her classes with Professor Wood. She was starting to feel better about completing a motivating project and was personally interested in the direction she was shifting toward.

She hadn't seen Darby since the evening she went out with Nic, but she did receive a thumbs up at some point during the night of their date. She was hoping that Nic finally came to his senses and realized how lucky he would be to date such a good person, and that his Casanova persona would change.

Sam struggled to sleep late in the morning since her body was so accustomed to early calls at the studio, and Sunday morning was no exception. Rolling over, she checked her faithful day planner and saw that she had marked off time on her calendar to sit down with her mom and go over all the finances.

Hmmmmm, she thought, *I'll need a double shot of caffeine if I am going to tackle that project today. Actually, I may need something stronger than caffeine.*

Sam didn't smell the aroma of freshly brewed coffee, and the house was still quiet, so she thought she would again take the opportunity to get in an early morning jog before her mom woke up, and she confronted the overdue bills and lack of income issues.

Quickly pulling on a pair of running shorts and a sports bra, Sam braided her hair and grabbed a hat. Picking up her running shoes, she tiptoed down the hall and quietly let herself out the front door.

She put her shoes on and started her regular stretching routine on the front porch when she heard a car start up down the street. Sam turned towards the noise and realized that it was a remarkably familiar silver Toyota with a catchy little sticker on the bumper. *You have got to be kidding me*, Sam thought to herself. *That's Dolly Bunosky's car leaving Mr. Fletcher's house! Ewww!*

Edwin Fletcher had lived across the street and a couple of houses down from the Martin women for as long as Sam could remember. Sam thought he took extra time and effort to make sure he knew where they were going, when they were away from home, and when they had visitors. On a good day, she reasoned that he was just trying to be protective of the two single women, and she had to admit that it was nice to know that someone was watching out for them. On a bad day, she found herself ducking for cover when she saw him headed her way, or at the very least, running right by him like she never saw him.

Silver-haired with a neatly trimmed white beard and rimless glasses, he could have passed for Santa if he wasn't the size of an elf. Sam had learned over the years to stay on his good side because he could be very persistent if you happened to leave your garbage can on the curb too long or let your grass grow just a quarter of an inch higher than the HOA regulations. Sam figured that most of the originals in the neighborhood, like Mr. Fletcher, were retired and were just trying to make sure that their beloved neighborhood stayed upmarket. Not that there were that many originals left.

Sam headed out to run in the opposite direction of the Fletcher residence because the last thing that she wanted to do was witness the old man standing on his front porch in his boxers or tighty whities. She wasn't sure she could handle spying him blowing kisses goodbye to his lady friend, the glow-in-the-dark dressing and artistically gifted, Dolly. She knew that some situations were simply better ignored, but it now made sense when Dolly told her that she had been with Edwin during their conversation at the studio. She just didn't realize that they were together, as in sharing sugar together. *Yikes*, she thought to herself. *How will I be able to look ol' Dolly in the eye when I see her again?* Running as fast as she could down the street so that no one accidentally spotted her, she started her workout.

Even though Sam had decided to run in the early morning hours, after completing her regular route through the neighborhood, she was soaked in sweat. It was almost like trying to jog in a sauna. The joys of living in Houston, Texas.

While she was jogging and doing her best thinking and problem-solving, she decided that the preeminent course of action was to confront her mom directly and ask her to show her all the paperwork concerning the house finances and her retirement savings. When she entered the house and was greeted with the smell of coffee and Judy's famous homemade apple kolaches, Sam's mouth began to water, and her stomach growled. She decided to quickly rinse off, change clothes, and then join her mom for breakfast before getting down to business.

At five feet nine inches tall and what some people would call an Amazon build, and with two more inches in height from her damp hair twisted on top of her head, Sam entered the kitchen wearing a soft old T-shirt dress, looking more like she was working the catwalk than a person relaxing on a Sunday morning. With her mouth ready, she sat down at the table and reached for one of the homemade pastries. The smell alone brought back so many memories of her and her mom making the dough and preparing the filling, but the delectable taste was enough to bring tears to her eyes.

Her mom's routine of making the German pastry had evolved into her making dozens at one time, with a variety of fruit toppings, and then freezing them for a special occasion. If there was a new or sick neighbor or an addition to a family, Judy would thaw out a plateful and take them over as a friendly gesture. This wasn't the same as making them together like in the old days, but the reheated tasty delicacy was just as good, and Sam and her sweet tooth could never resist them.

"I can't tell you how good this tastes. I'm glad that I already exercised today."

Judy snorted and said, "Seriously? You lead exercise classes for a living, and you have the body of Aphrodite. I think a couple of kolaches won't hurt a thing. Anyway, they have fruit in them. See the apples?"

Sam grinned, "I've always said everything in moderation, but I don't believe the filling in these kolaches counts for a serving of fruit." With her mouth full, she said, "I hope I didn't wake you when I went for my run this morning."

"No, no. I was just lying in bed and going through a few things in my head."

"Speaking of going through a few things, why don't we sit down together, and you can show me where you stand on finances?"

Judy's coffee mug was at her lips, and she narrowed her eyes as she took a long sip.

"I'm not trying to be nosy, Mom, so as you would say, don't get your panties in a wad, but don't you think it would be easier for you to share the basics of what's going on around here instead of letting me be surprised when the water or the power is just turned off?"

Judy winced a little bit and set her mug on the table. "It's not that I think you are being nosy. You know I don't have any real secrets from you. It's just that lately, I can't seem to get it together. It's embarrassing if nothing else."

Sam reached out and touched her mom's hand. "It's going to be fine, Mom, we can figure this all out. I'll clean up the kitchen, and you go get started in the office for us to go through everything."

Judy refilled her coffee mug and headed towards the office when she turned and said, "By the way, Dolly Bunosky called a few minutes ago and is coming by today to help me pick out new colors for the house. Isn't that neighborly of her?"

Sam smiled and nodded her head and thought to herself that she wasn't sure she would be able to live in a hot pink or lime green house. She finished that thought by noting that surely the homeowner's association would give the Dolly and Judy submission a hard no when they saw the crazy colors. *However,* she pondered, *I do know that she has some influence over the head of the committee.*

CHAPTER 11

Judy had always been a whiz at numbers. The small family-owned oil and gas company that she had been employed at for over twenty years made sure that her loyalty and devotion to the company and family were rewarded, or so Sam had always believed.

Judy was only fifty-eight years old, and up until she was laid off during the last downturn in the economy, she loved her job and coworkers. Weber Oil and Gas Company was a privately held oil and gas exploration enterprise, which took care of their employees like they were family.

Judy had an accounting degree from Texas A&M University, in College Station, Texas, and when she moved back to Houston after graduating, she went to work in the petroleum industry. At Weber, she processed oil and gas revenue payments to investors as well as maintained all the monthly oil and gas imbalances that were created due to owners not receiving their proportionate share of production for each offshore property. She was paid well and, along with her coworkers, was given a small percentage of the royalties in each investment fund that the company managed as an alternative way to provide for the employee's retirement.

Regardless, after sitting and going through all the paper-work that Judy had in her old black vertical metal filing cabinet, Sam had yet to see anything that resembled an IRA, 401(K), or any type of personal retirement plan for that matter.

"Mom, are you sure you didn't accidentally get rid of some of the paperwork that had your retirement informa-tion on it when you were cleaning this office out last week?'

"Yes, I'm sure. I was very careful with what got shredded and went out to the recycle bin."

"Okay, then let's look at your computer. Can you show me your banking information and how you pay your bills?"

"That's easy, I just log in to my bank, and it shows me what I have in savings and what I have in checking. See?"

Sam watched as her mom logged into her personal bank account and then tried not to sound panicked as she sput-tered, "Is this all of your savings? That's your retirement account as well?"

There were two balances in Judy's name. One was a regular checking account, and the other one was labeled a money market account. The balances that were in the two accounts made Sam's hands start to sweat. If this was indeed all the funds that Judy had left to her name, they were in some serious trouble. The only positive aspect of this discovery was that maybe Judy wasn't forgetting to pay the bills, maybe she just *couldn't* pay all the bills.

"No, no. While I was working, I put any money that I received from the funds into a separate account. That was the company's way of supporting our retirement."

"Ok, this is good. Where is *that* account?" Sam asked as she felt her anxiety levels drop slightly.

Judy bit her lower lip and looked off into the distance. "You're going to think I am really slipping, but I set up that account with the help of our company's finance manager. He was a genius when it came to investments, and he assured me that when I was ready to retire, this investment account would be a nice little nest egg. The way it was set up, my extra earnings from the company's oil and gas revenues were sent directly to this account for investing. He managed the whole thing and gave me all the login information for my account."

Sam started to sweat again because she knew Judy was talking about Bill Bernhardt. Mr. Bernhardt had been pushing up daisies for years now, and with the dissolution of the entire company, Sam wasn't sure where to start for help in finding this mystery account.

"So, you do know what bank or financial company holds this account, right? Or you don't?" Sam said, trying to keep her voice calm.

"Of course, I know where it is. Bill, God rest his soul, had everything set up on my old laptop, but when the company closed, I stopped using that laptop and just started using my desktop computer."

"Now we're getting somewhere. Log in and let's look at your investment account."

Sam watched as Judy navigated the mouse to the search bar and typed in MoneyTreeCoins. She had never heard of a bank with that name, but she wasn't in the finance world, and she barely had enough pennies to keep in her local bank, much less an international institution.

When she got to the homepage, Judy typed in her username and her password, and they both stared at the screen waiting for MoneyTreeCoins to open her account information. The green coin icon flipped from front to back several times, and an error message appeared that said either the username or the password was incorrect, along with a statement that said you had four more attempts before the account was locked.

Now Sam's hands and brow started to sweat. "Are you sure you have the correct user ID and password?"

"Yes, and I know that the username is my email address. Let me try just one more time, maybe I typed the password wrong."

"What's the password?"

Judy waved her hand and said, "That's easy, all my passwords are the same."

Sam made a mental head slap as well as a mental note to help Judy update all her passwords and said, "So you know that's a no-no, right, Mom?"

"I know it's not what you are supposed to do, but trying to remember all the passwords for everything that I log into is just too much."

Again, Judy typed in the password, and they both held their breath as the coin icon again flipped from front to back for several seconds. Sam didn't realize she was holding her breath until the screen changed and Judy Martin's home page appeared on the screen.

Sam was so happy that she let out a little, "Whoohooo!"

Judy smiled and looked a little smug as she said, "I told you I knew the login information."

The homepage was divided into several sections that included graphs, pricing on different stocks, a market update segment that had the latest news on cryptocurrency, and Judy's MoneyTreeCoins address.

Sam looked at the screen and asked, "This isn't regular stock, like on the New York Stock Exchange, is it, Mom?"

"No, dear. You know I have always been good at numbers, but Bill was exceptional when it came to investments and finance. At first, he had my funds invested in some mutual funds, but then he came to me one day and told me that he had put all his money into MoneyTreeCoins. He highly recommended that I do the same. He said that he could set everything up for me, and we could transfer the money in the mutual funds retirement account to this cryptocurrency account."

"Mom, you might as well be speaking Greek to me. I have no idea how any of this works. Where is the balance in this account?"

"Hmmmmm, let me see," Judy murmured. She moved the mouse around and clicked on a wallet icon.

Sam's eyes popped open, and she leaned closer to the screen to make sure that she wasn't seeing things. The account total was close to one million dollars.

"Oh, wow! This is great! You're going to be fine. You could pay off the mortgage on the house and still have money left over for your retirement."

Judy squinted her eyes at Sam and said, "I'm not that old and senile yet. I don't know if I am ready for retirement."

"No, of course, Mom. I just meant that you have *options*. Why don't we transfer some of that money or crypto-money or whatever it's called over to your bank, and we can get you caught up on all the bills?"

They both turned their heads to look back at the screen in silence. After a few seconds of stillness, Sam said, "You do know how to access this account, right?"

Judy clicked on the help tab and typed in how to transfer funds from your wallet. A screen popped up that instructed her to go to her personal wallet and enter her key for further options on opening her personal cyber savings account.

"Mom, do you have a key of some sort to this account?"

"Well, I've never actually accessed any of this money. I guess I have some sort of key or password that I used when Bill set this account up. Let me think about this while I get ready for Dolly Bunosky to come over."

"Wait, what? She's coming over *now*? I thought you meant later in the day, and don't you think this is more important?" Sam sputtered.

"When Dolly called this morning, she said she would be happy to come right over and help me pick out a color combination for the house that would be stunning and impressive for our little cottage. I am going to run and pick up a few more paint colors. I want her to have plenty to work with so that we can select a beautiful color combination. She practically guaranteed me that it would meet the GOOF homeowner's association guidelines and get approved in no time."

Sam thought to herself, *I will not think about how Ms. Bunosky can guarantee that.*

CHAPTER 12

Sam worked on her marketing project for the rest of the afternoon and stayed well hidden in her bedroom while her mom and Ms. Bunosky discussed paint colors and combinations in the kitchen and the backyard. She was feeling very satisfied with how far she had come and the research she was able to accomplish. She decided that she could kill two birds with one stone and make good on her promise to have dinner with Leo, even if it was sooner than they had discussed. She also planned on getting him to explain cryptocurrency to her. He should certainly be able to enlighten her on just exactly what her mom had invested in all those years ago, as well as, hopefully, advise her on what she needed to do with that money now. After checking her day planner just to make sure that she was truly available, she sent Leo a text.

Hi, would you be open to an early dinner tonight?

She waited while the three little dots were dancing, and he sent a reply.

Would love to, belle âme.

Sam's stomach did a little flutter, and she bounced into the bathroom. She was almost always dressed in workout clothes and tennis shoes when Leo saw her, so she decided that today she would put forth a little extra effort. Sam added some light makeup, and she wound her now clean and dry hair into a topknot. She put on some white jeans and an off-the-shoulder blouse that was embroidered with flowers in the style of a Mexican peasant top.

She was just adjusting her long tassel earrings when she heard voices coming from the front of the house. She took one final look at herself and headed out to the den, where Judy was talking to Leo.

Leo took in Sam with one long appraising look and walked forward to give her cheek a light kiss. Sam smiled and turned to Judy and said, "Mom, you are welcome to come with us."

Leo said, "I just said the same thing to mon amie."

"You two go and have a good time. Leo, try to get her to put her day planner away and relax this evening. Dolly and I came up with some great combinations today. I'm going to paint some of her ideas on the back of the house so I can get a better picture of the end results."

Sam glanced at the kitchen table and could see all the sample cans of paint and color swatches on top of a layer of newspaper. She could feel her anxiety start to rise again just thinking about what the neighbors were going to say when they saw their house doused in blazing yellow with parfait pink trim, or some other equally loud combination.

Leo followed her gaze and said, "I feel like there is a story here that I can't wait to hear. Judy, it was good to see you."

Sam followed Leo out of the house, and he opened the car door for her to slide inside.

As he walked around the front of the car, she couldn't help but admire just how good-looking he was in his dark jeans and cool white linen shirt with the sleeves rolled up. He could have worn something from a clothing donation store and still looked good. It had to be the way that he carried himself—self-confident and composed with a little bit of coolness.

They drove in silence as they headed to Crisp, a local neighborhood gastropub that was one of their favorite places to spend time.

Sam was feeling somewhat relieved after finding her mom's retirement account and getting her marketing project better organized and on track for completion. She would worry about all the appointments she needed to get her mom to starting tomorrow. Tonight, she was going to share Leo's yolo and devil-may-care attitude.

"You're quiet tonight, ma belle."

Sam turned and looked out the window and said, "I think I am just happy to be out of the house and not at school, work, or dealing with some other chore that needs my attention."

"I've always said that you are not having nearly enough fun in your life, and I'm glad that you texted me about dinner. I take it you had an opening in your schedule?"

She glanced over at him at this last statement and saw the sexy little smirk on his face.

"You know I love a full schedule."

Leo caught her eye and said, "Pencil me in any time you have an opening. I can always think of something for us to do."

Sam squirmed a little in her leather seat and tried to pretend that she didn't catch his double meaning. *And this is why I can't get serious with you,* she said to herself, *You can turn me into a girl with yo-yo panties!*

When they were seated in a corner booth and the waiter had brought Sam a glass of wine and Leo a St. Arnold's beer, a Houston local brew, he reached across the table and took her hand.

"What has been keeping you so busy lately? So busy that you can't even take an evening off to relax a little. I guess it goes without saying that I was pleasantly surprised to get your text earlier."

Sam decided to get the business part of the date behind her, and then maybe she really could unwind and appreciate the time she had with this handsome and oh so persuasive man.

"Leo, what do you know about cryptocurrency?"

Leo let out a little laugh and said, "Whoa, whoa, whoa. Is this a friendly dinner or a finance class? Are you thinking that you want to dabble in digital money?"

Sam squinted her eyes and tilted her head. "Are you saying you don't know anything about cryptocurrency, or are you just giving me a hard time to irritate my sweet disposition?

Leo reached across the table and grabbed her hand. "I'm just teasing you, Sam. I'll be happy to tell you what I know but tell me why this is coming up. The last time we talked about money, you were hoping the Booger had a few more good years in her. All I am saying is that I didn't know you had the extra funds for unpredictable cryptocurrency investments, or are you trying to hit the lottery, so to speak, with your studio savings?"

Sam had to smile. With Leo's French accent, the Booger always sounded like the Burger. He was charming and fun, and she didn't know why she couldn't just let herself be swept away, and as her Aunt Pookie would say, enjoy some of that sweet sugar.

She sighed and then gave Leo all the details of the MoneyTreeCoins account that her mom had shown her that morning. When Sam got to the end of her story, she noticed that he was no longer smiling. In fact, he looked very serious.

"Sam, I will be happy to do some research on MoneyTreeCoins for you. I do know that it is one of the more recognized cryptocurrencies on the web, and there is a crypto exchange where you can buy and sell your online assets. There are some well-known currencies, such as Helium, Cagecoin, and Exponential. It is becoming increasingly popular, and I dare to say mainstream, but it can still be very volatile and perhaps too risky for Judy's retirement fund. I am assuming your mom has her funds in a crypto wallet where she can access her virtual money?"

"I only know what I saw when Mom logged in this morning. She definitely has a personal account that displays a dollar amount associated with it, but I have no idea how to access those funds. And, from what I saw this morning, neither does she."

"It's all supposed to be very safe and secure. It's designed to be exceedingly difficult to be hacked on the internet, and there are several security features in place, including what I believe is your own personal code or key, so to speak. To be able to access your money, you must input this complex key that matches a company key."

Sam tried not to think about where this personal key might be to access the account and said with a questioning glance, "You know, maybe it would just be easier to get a password reset or get rekeyed?"

"Very cute play on words there, mon amie, and I will do some research, but I do believe that once your private key is gone, you are just out of luck. Whatever is in your crypto wallet is gone. Fini!"

Sam looked up, caught the waiter's eye, and touched the rim of her now empty wine glass. Leo caught the signal and tapped his beer mug as well.

"Look, let's enjoy the rest of the evening, and I will do some digging this week on MoneyTreeCoins and cryptocurrency. Now why don't we switch topics, and you tell me why your mom's kitchen table looked like a paint store?"

Sam had Leo laughing, or maybe it was the two beers, as she told him about getting the new paint colors for the house approved through GOOF, Mr. Fletcher and his romance with Dolly Bunosky, and her predilection for colors that could sting the eyes. Sam couldn't bring herself to disclose her mom's memory fog and the upcoming medical tests that she needed to have to find the underlying cause of her problem. Sam knew he would listen and be thoughtful when she was ready to discuss the issue, but she just wasn't there yet.

Sam was thoroughly enjoying herself, and they finished off their favorite Cluck You BBQ hand-tossed pizza that combined candied jalapeños, beer can chicken, and barbeque sauce to create a mouthwatering taste sensation.

"Do you want some dessert? We could have a nightcap at a bar, or we could go to my apartment and watch the sunset on the patio?"

Sam sighed and decided that it wouldn't hurt to have one evening that didn't involve her research project, faulty memories, arabesque pulses at the gym, or financial constraints. "As long as you promise me that we won't talk about crypto dollars and paint colors, I would love to see the sunset."

"Ma belle, I don't believe there will be a lot of talking," he smiled and held out his hand to help her up.

Sam felt her stomach start to flutter and thought to herself that there was a real possibility that there would be some sugar-sharing tonight.

CHAPTER 13

The following day, by the time Sam had made it down I-10, or the Katy Freeway as Houstonians called it, and exited Studewood, she began to breathe easier. Tardiness was not an option since she needed to be at the studio in time to set up all the class implements, get her music keyed up and her mic on, and be ready to greet her clients as they arrived for class.

Darby was barre tending at the check-in desk when Sam made it to the studio to prepare for one of her favorite classes, Burning Barre Buns.

"Hello, stranger. How is it going, and how was your date with Nic a couple of days ago?"

Darby looked at Sam with a Mona Lisa smile and said, "Well, my momma would say that I have fallen for him faster than a knife fight in a phone booth. He's sweet and kind, and we had a great time getting to talk without all his gaming groupies and friends hanging around."

"If you're happy, then I'm happy. When are you supposed to see him again?"

"He's actually coming by the studio when I get off work, and we are going to watch the bats take flight at sunset tonight."

Sam held in a grimace and didn't think that was such a great idea for a date, but she knew it was a Houston tradition. It is quite the display to watch the bat colony that resided under the Waugh bridge near downtown take flight each evening for their nightly feeding. Not her concept of a lovely, relaxing evening, but to each their own, she supposed.

Sam gave a little grin and said, "What do you wear to a bat-feeding frenzy?"

"You know I can help you with that! Something bright that will make you stand out in the waning daylight."

They both jumped a little because they didn't realize Dolly Bunosky had come into the studio and was sitting on a bench quietly putting on her sticky socks, and listening to everything that they had said. In one of her signature ensembles, Judy had squeezed herself into a pair of shiny royal blue leggings, a coordinating exercise bra that peeked out from a tie-dyed tank top that had printed on it, "I don't like to brag but I'm hot!"

"Hello, Ms. Bunosky. I'm sorry we didn't hear you come in."

"That's fine, dear. I know this isn't my usual class time, but I have some stiff muscles that I need to stretch."

Sam did a mental head shake and bit her tongue so as not to ask in any way, shape, or form as to why her muscles were sore. No way did she want to hear about any acrobatic moves that she may or may not have been trying out with Mr. Fletcher.

Darby asked, "Thank you for the suggestion, Ms. Bunosky. I'll keep you posted on what I end up wearing to watch the bats take flight. Now, I have you all checked in so you can go back to the studio when you are ready."

"Thank you, Darby. And Sam, your mom and I got the new house colors narrowed down to a few exciting combinations. I do have an eye for the aesthetically pleasing. You will also be happy to know that she had the paperwork for the Neighborhood Watch program filled out and was going to walk it over to Edwin's house when I left. As soon as she makes up her mind which paint combo she likes, she is going to turn in that paperwork for approval with GOMO." She leaned forward towards Sam conspiratorially and whispered, "You know Edwin is going to help her get her submissions accepted. He is such a lovely man."

Again, Sam had to bite her tongue not to come right out and say, *ewwww*. Maybe she needed to take another hard look at Mr. Fletcher, the overly observant neighbor and former Marine, but really, she couldn't get past his unbuttoned overalls.

"Thank you so much for helping her, I'm sure the house is going to look fantastic," Sam said with a forced smile.

Darby was listening to this exchange, and her eyeballs had gotten bigger and bigger. When Dolly sauntered into the studio, Darby said in a voice just loud enough for Sam to hear, "Well, butter my butt and call me a biscuit, but I do believe from hearing that conversation that you are going to have one fine new paint job on your momma's house."

Sam just looked at her friend and rolled her eyes.

CHAPTER 14

Aunt Pookie showed up at the house on Lamonte Lane the following day, dressed in a chartreuse jumpsuit that was belted at the waist with a multicolored silk scarf. She had rolled the legs up to mid-calf so that her sparkly Converse high tops were completely visible. Her signature hair was razored short on the back and sides with a long bang that she artfully dyed a deep magenta and gelled into place. People who met her frequently commented that she gave the impression of an aging and even more flamboyant David Bowie. Sam knew that comparison amused and delighted her aunt.

When Sam opened the front door to let her inside, she leaned in to give her their traditional kiss-kiss greeting.

"Hi, Aunt Pookie. I'm sorry that I couldn't get a hold of you earlier to go over Mom's doctor's visit, but I'm so glad you are here now." She paused for a breath and then added, "I want to give you all the details, but I'm really hoping that I can get you to take her to one or some of her follow-up tests?"

"Darlin', that's exactly why I am here. I was hoping that I could catch up with you, see what I can do to lend a hand, and peek at these paint colors that Judy wanted me to look over."

Sam's eyes grew wide, and she glanced around the small house to see where her mom was hiding. Sam realized when she didn't see her anywhere in the den and kitchen area of the small home that she must be out in the backyard working on her paint selections or working in a flowerbed before the temperature outside was too much to handle.

Good grief, Sam thought to herself, B*etween Dolly Bunosky and Aunt Pookie's input, this tiny house is absolutely going to attract attention. Maybe just not the kind that Mom was hoping for.* There was no way that either one of these *artistic* ladies could pick a color that was subtly and naturally occurring in nature, as the GOMO requested. Well, she was going to let those chips fall where they may. Sam just didn't have the time or energy to fight all these ladies about proper paint colors for the house.

"Let me grab my day planner and see if any of Mom's follow-up appointments will fit into your schedule. I do appreciate your help. I already have it down in my planner to take her for her EEG, but her MRI is this afternoon in the Medical Center, and I'm working on getting someone to cover my classes so that I can take her down there," Sam said as she reached for her backpack.

"My dear, you know you don't have to shoulder this responsibility on your own. I'm always available."

As the only child of her single mother, Sam always knew that she would have full responsibility for her mom's well-being and care when she reached her golden years. She just never imagined that those years would start so soon, and she couldn't see that there was anything golden about them right now.

Sam updated her planner and penciled in Aunt Pookie to take her sister for her bloodwork appointment and the afternoon MRI, which Pookie insisted that she could do to free up Sam for work. By the time they got all the appointments squared away and Pookie informed of the details of what Dr. Chen had covered with them, Judy had let herself into the kitchen from the backdoor, letting in a noticeable swath of balmy air with her. Wearing her old garden gloves and a wide-brimmed straw hat, she sat down at the kitchen table with a perspiring red face and a muumuu that was doing little to keep her cool.

Sam walked over, opened the refrigerator, and handed her mom a bottle of water. "Mom, I hope you are hydrating enough while you are out gardening, or painting, or whatever you are doing. It's too hot to be working outside unless it's earlier in the morning or late in the evening."

"Little sister, listen to your angel. We can't have you having a heat stroke in this Houston sauna."

Judy looked over at her sister and smiled as she said, "It's good to see you, too, Pook. I was just getting some of the weeds pulled where I painted my test colors so that you can get a good, clean look at how this old girl is going to look with her makeover. Let me know when you are ready to brave the heat and humidity, and I will take you on a tour. Sam, why don't you come outside for a vote as well?"

"Um, no, Mom. I'm going to leave the paint selection process to the professionals."

Sam left the two sisters discussing paint colors and wandered back to her room, where she started to gather her daily necessities for school and work. She was reaching for her backpack and a hat to give her some sun protection when she heard her phone pinging that she had a new text message.

Ma belle, I have done some research on MoneyTreeCoins. Do you have time for a quick lunch? Or a drink after work?

Sam knew it would be cutting it close, but she could meet Leo after she finished teaching her last class and before she needed to be at her evening marketing class in the downtown area. She wouldn't be able to have a drink, but she would be able to listen to what Leo had to say about the crypto account and possibly get some information on how to transfer some of the money to her mom's checking account.

Can we meet after I finish teaching my last class and before I head downtown?

Sam thought the smiley face that she added at the end of her text was enough to let him know she was grateful for the help, and because she didn't add the little kissy face, he would know this meeting was purely for business.

As Sam headed towards the front door, she could hear Aunt Pookie talking to her mom in the small kitchen, "It's not a big deal, Judy. Sam is going to be fine. I know you want her dreams to come true even more than she does, and we both know that she runs herself over hell's half acre every day working on making them happen."

Sam felt a little guilty, but she slowed down to hear what her mom had to say about that comment.

"You're right. I need to follow through with these appointments and get myself together so that not only can I figure out what to do with myself, but also so that Sam can stop hovering about and worrying about me all day every day. I don't know if I should feel loved or annoyed that she is like an ant on a sugar mound running to work and school and back to the house every chance she gets."

Sam decided she had better speak up as she rounded the corner in the kitchen. "Mom, I'm sorry that I just overheard what you and Aunt Pookie were saying, but I'm fine, and I just want to help you get better. Some good news, I'm meeting up with Leo before class tonight to talk to him about your crypto account."

Aunt Pookie batted her eyes and got a big smile on her face. "Please tell me this is for more pleasure than it is for business, and what is this crypto account that you are talking about?"

"Mom has a retirement account, or, um, an investment account, which was set up when she worked at Weber Oil and Gas. Um, I think she may have forgotten about it or was distracted by everything going on around here, and we are trying to figure out how to access the money so she can get caught up on the bills."

Sam slid her eyes to her mom to see how she was taking this statement and saw that she had a funny, faraway look on her face.

"What, Mom? What's wrong? I wasn't trying to point out your forgetfulness or embarrass you."

"No, no, I was just thinking when you said that about Weber Oil and Gas, that I used to be able to access that account on my old work computer. Maybe the key or password is stored on that laptop."

Aunt Pookie said, "Are you saying that you have an account that you are trying to get into, and you can't remem . . . I mean, you are not sure where the money is located?"

Judy was nodding her head yes and still staring off into oblivion. She quietly said to herself, "I'm sure that I still have that laptop in my box from work when the company closed. They were nice enough to allow us to take them for our own personal use, but I already had my desktop computer here in the office. I've never used it, or anything else that was in that old box, for that matter."

"I tell you what, darlin'," Pookie drawled, "let's let Sam get to work. How about we look at those paint colors, and then you and I can go through that old workbox and dig out that computer and look for passwords and whatnot. Problem solved."

Sam gave her mom a kiss on the cheek. "See, this is all going to work out fine. I've got to run, but I'll text you the address and information for her MRI appointment, Aunt Pook. I'll check on you later, Mom."

"You do not need to check on me later! That's exactly what I'm talking about."

Aunt Pookie adjusted her scarf at her waist and said, "Go on, Sam. Judy and I will be right as rain. You be sure and give that cutie some extra attention."

Sam walked out the front door and thought to herself, *Thank goodness for Aunt Pook, and I promise myself that I will not blink an eye when the house is painted like a kindergartener's finger-painting project.*

CHAPTER 15

Sam loaded the Booger with everything she would need for the day and headed towards the studio. She had promised Cara that she would help her go through some of the applicants for a part-time barre tender position they had open. If she could quickly go through the prospective employee applications and resumes and teach her scheduled classes, she should have plenty of time left during the day to start finalizing her marketing project. She was happy with the goals and ideas that had developed as the project progressed. If she could finish the assignment and get that checked off her to-do list, she would feel better, and then she could concentrate on what she needed to do to help get her mother's life straight, both mentally and financially.

Cara Womack was at the front desk when Sam walked inside to start her day. She was a little taken aback that Darby wasn't there managing the reception duties, and Cara must have seen the confusion on Sam's face.

"Darby called and said she would be in later. Something about a water leak at their apartment, so I am here covering for her until she can make it in."

Cara was in her mid-thirties with two children in elementary school and a husband who worked in the oil and gas industry as a petroleum engineer. That wasn't anything unusual, as the Houston metro area had the largest concentration of petrochemical engineering in the world. It seemed like everyone you talked to worked in the oil and gas industry or had a relative, spouse, or friend who either worked in the sector or in a business that supported the energy-related enterprise. What was unusual and impressive was the fact that Cara was able to run the studio, be a full-time mom and wife, volunteer at the kid's school, and be a long-time member of the Special Children's Committee at the Houston Livestock Show and Rodeo, the largest livestock exhibition and rodeo in the world, and still always look fresh and invigorated. Sam wasn't sure how she managed to juggle her schedule and wear all her many hats, cowboy one included, but Sam admired her calm demeanor, her success and dedication to her family, and her social concerns.

"I'm going to get the studio set up for the next class, review my planned workout, and then maybe we can go through some of those applications for the barre tender position?"

"You go ahead and get everything prepped, and I'll get the stack of applicants that I have already combed through, and then we can get your take on them."

While Sam was setting out the rubber bands and exercise balls, she could hear Cara talking. It was a little early for students to be coming in, but you never could tell if someone just wanted to get there ahead of the scheduled class time to secure their favorite spot in the studio or just to get in some extra stretching before class started.

When the setup was complete, she walked back towards the check-in desk and saw that Darby had made it to work. Cara and Darby were looking at the online work schedule, and Sam wandered over to look over their shoulders.

"Hi, Darby. Is everything okay?"

Darby jumped, and her hand flew to her chest. "You gave me a start! I didn't see the Booger in the back lot."

Sam thought that Darby seemed a little jumpy or guilty or both and answered her with, "I was blocked from pulling in the back when I got here by a yard maintenance truck and trailer, so I parked on the street in front. What's going on at your apartment?"

"I was just telling Cara that our water heater was leaking, and the landlord scheduled today with no notice to have the plumbers come and replace the tank. I had to go by a friend's house to get ready for work."

Sam cut her eyes towards Cara, who was taking this statement in with little reaction, and then looked back at Darby, who at least had the good sense not to look her in the eye.

"Um, really? You know you can always come by my house if you need a place to stay *or* shower."

Cara, being the ultimate in smoothness and composure and sensing that this was where she needed to step back from this personal conversation, calmly said, "Darby, now that you are here, I'm going to leave the front desk to you, and Sam, come see me when you can talk about those applicants."

Darby and Sam waited in silence as Cara let herself into her office and then shut the door.

Sam swung around and faced Darby. "Please tell me that apartment did not belong to a friend named Nic!"

Darby immediately protested, "No, no, it wasn't like that at all! He's been very nice, and when he heard that my place didn't have any water, he volunteered his apartment for me to shower and get dressed. He wasn't even there!"

Sam let that statement hang in the air for a few seconds and then decided to take the high road instead of letting her mind think that her sweet friend was using the needy Southern belle method to attract a boyfriend, or even worse, the I'm throwing myself at you approach. Sam had witnessed both methods in action since she was in junior high, and to this day, could still not stomach the approaches. The helpless routine was just not in her genetic makeup, and if her mother or Aunt Pookie had ever seen her putting on such a fake show, they would have been the first ones to laugh at such a ridiculous attempt at phony helplessness. As for throwing herself at a man for attention, Sam hoped that she would always have way too much pride and self-respect for that strategy.

"Well, okay, I guess that was nice of him." Sam waited a couple of seconds before adding, "Just out of curiosity, how is his apartment? Does he have a solid gold toilet?"

Darby's face started to redden as she started to smile. "It was so much nicer than my place with all my roommates running in and out and our mismatched, second-hand furniture, that's for sure. I really didn't look in any of his drawers or cabinets if that's what you were thinking! I am not going to be one of those people!"

Darby hesitated for a moment before slyly adding, "What I can tell you is that his shower was spotless, and he had all the Kiehl's products for men on his countertop. I believe he has more hair gels, face creams, and moisturizers than I do."

"So, do you think he's exceptionally neat, or do you think his daddy sends over a housekeeper to take care of Junior every week?"

Darby laughed and said, "Definitely a housekeeper. I don't think that man has hit a lick in years unless you consider computer gaming work."

"Well, there you go, at least you see the real Nic." Sam started to ease towards the office and said, "I need to get with Cara and go over some resumes. Come and get me if it gets too crazy up here."

Sam spent the rest of the morning and early afternoon teaching her classes and reviewing resumes. She had her regular clients that she could always count on and several new ones that made teaching class a juggling act between spending all the class time instructing the newer students on correct form and posture and making sure that the veterans still got a challenging set. It was always nice to know before class started what the breakdown of clients was between seasoned regulars versus self-conscious newbies, but Sam usually had to get this information herself. As she was wiping down the equipment after the third class, Darby wandered into the studio and started helping with the cleanup process.

"How's your project coming along? Are you ready to present it to your professor and class?"

"I don't think I told you, but I tweaked the focus of my presentation from marketing a typical barre studio."

Darby raised her dark eyebrows and said, "Really, how did you tweak it?"

Sam thought about it for a second and said, "Just something that I have been completely oblivious to. I'll let you read it when I get it finished and get your input on my oral presentation."

Sam and Darby had gotten into the habit of using each other as a sounding board, proofreader, simulated audience, and editor for all their projects since they were both on a marketing track degree program. Sam was further into her degree plan and closer to graduating, but it was good to have Darby's input, who was intuitive, and sharp, and would not hesitate to call donkey dung when Sam's work was below par.

When the studio was clean and the sound equipment was stowed away, they both headed back to the entry and reception desk area. Darby went behind the check-in area, and Sam indicated that she was going to work on her coursework in the office until it was time to head to campus.

"Look, if your water problems aren't magically resolved when you get home, please know that you can come to stay with me. Anytime."

"Well, bless your heart, what would I do without you?" Darby said as she chuckled.

"You won't have to ever find out, sister-friend."

Sam continued researching the final details of her marketing project for the remainder of the afternoon. She was feeling pretty satisfied with her efforts and decided it was time to get herself together to go meet Leo for their quick drink. She was going to have to order a virgin margarita, or in her book, green, sad juice, but she thought to herself, *I'm going to get Mom's financial*

situation straightened out and her memory fog resolved,
and then I am going to drink one or three large glasses of
green, happy juice.

Sam went into the bathroom and applied a healthy dose of deodorant and body spray, brushed her teeth and her hair, smeared some lip gloss on her lips, and dabbed some bronzer on her cheeks. "I'm not doing all of this for Leo," she reflected aloud. "I am doing this because I am a strong and confident woman who likes to look her best." *Who was she fooling?* she laughed to herself. She was most certainly trying to look her best because she was going to see Leo. She knew he was around smart, well-dressed women every day at his office who didn't always smell like they had just taken a whore's bath in the gym sink. "One day," she muttered to herself, "I am going to be calm and collected and have all the time in the world to meet some-one after work. And not in workout leggings. And with fresh, clean armpits."

She went back into the office and reloaded her old backpack, checked her day planner to make sure she hadn't forgotten anything, and then headed to the recep-tion area.

Darby was checking in another class, and Sam waved at her as she hurried out the front door and headed towards the Booger. Sam and Leo had agreed on the bar at El Torero for their quick drink and information exchange about the cryptocurrency account. The restaurant was a Houston establishment that was well known for its excellent Tex-Mex food, and more importantly, for its famous margaritas that only took one to require an Uber ride home.

When she pulled into the parking lot of the restaurant off Washington Avenue, a beaming valet greeted her as he held her door. Sam wasn't sure if he was grinning to be nice or if he was holding in a laugh at the Booger that he was about to valet park. *Again,* she thought to herself, *One day I'm also going to have a car that valets will fight over to park, or at least not be embarrassed to be seen parking.* She hurried into the reception area and did a quick scan of the restaurant. When she realized she had beaten Leo to their appointment, she told the host that she didn't need a table. After scoping out the interior, she snagged a high-top table at the rear of the bar area and ordered a frozen margarita with salt for Leo and a sans-alcohol version for herself.

While she was waiting for Leo and their drinks, she pulled out her day planner and her phone from her back-pack to check for any messages that might need her attention. When she didn't see anything from her mother, she decided to send her a quick text just to make sure that she was fine.

Hey! Meeting with Leo before class tonight. How was your MRI appointment today?

Sam waited a few seconds to see if the three dancing dots appeared, but she was distracted from that maddening activity when the waiter brought the drinks to the table. As he was placing them on the coasters, Sam felt a hand on her shoulder and a slight squeeze, and then Leo placed a light peck on her cheek.

Sam smiled, and Leo sat down across from her. "Belle, I'm sorry that I am late. You look beautiful as always."

Sam couldn't help herself, but one look at Leo's gorgeous face and hair and the way he wore his business suit and Italian loafers, and her lower stomach began to start a little salsa dancing.

Geez, she thought, w*hy does he have to be nice and look like that as well?*

"I'm sorry to rush this drink, but I have about thirty minutes before I have to leave for class. Can you tell me what you found out about MoneyTreeCoins?"

"Of course, ma belle. I did some digging into the background of the company and found that it was started in 2007 by an anonymous group that call themselves Juyo Don, which means main money in Korean."

"Okay, so what does that mean for Mom?"

"Nothing really, except that it is a commonly talked-about theory in the financial world that this secretive group is really just one individual. Nonetheless, it is a well-established company in the cryptocurrency world."

Leo continued to explain that there was a marketplace called a crypto exchange that allowed people to buy or sell their coins using different currencies. He also started to go into significant detail about the digital wallet that each user owns, where their coins are stored either in the cloud or on a hard drive on a computer. As Sam began losing focus on the details that Leo was going into, she decided she should cut to the chase.

"So essentially, you are telling me that the account is for real, and Mom just needs to access her wallet?" Sam commented, making air quotes when she said the word wallet.

"Oh yes, the money is for real, but it can be very volatile. It is a mostly unregulated business, and some people use its anonymity to participate in illegal activities. If this is Judy's retirement or life savings, I would recommend that she put it in something more traditional and secure."

"Okay, so the bottom line is, figure out how to access her account with her secret key since her coins are stored in the cloud. Right?"

"I have not seen her account or how it is set up, but from what you are telling me, it would seem like that would be the next logical step, bella," he confirmed.

"Spoken like a true lawyer."

Leo chuckled and said, "I have been trying to sound more professional in my statements, but I cannot seem to grasp the use of the Southern lingo that I am expected to incorporate into my vocabulary . . . um, I recon."

Sam almost spit her virgin margarita out laughing and said, "That would be, reckon, not recon. Recon is a mission, reckon is what you think."

"See, you think learning French is hard, but I assure you it is nothing like the Texan English that I have been trying to master for years."

"It's okay, you look cute no matter how you destroy our beautiful southern phrases and words."

Leo sat up straighter, arched his one eyebrow, and said, "You think I'm cute, huh?"

"Yes, but not right now. I have to get to class, and your cuteness is not going to make me late," Sam said between slurping up the last of her sad green juice and licking the last of the salt from the rim of the glass.

"Let me check my calendar, and I can get back to you on when I can take you to dinner to thank you for helping me with my mom's account."

Leo reached for her hand and said, "There's no need for that, but you let me know when you are available, and I *reckon* I will be there."

"See, I'm going to turn you into a Southerner, yet."

CHAPTER 16

After Sam had turned in her final outline and a synopsis of her proposed project to Professor Wood in class and was back in the Booger headed home, she thought that she should try and reach out to Aunt Pookie and get the details on how the MRI appointment had gone that day.

Thank goodness that her aunt was able to go with her mom. Not necessarily because she thought she wouldn't be able to find the medical center in Houston, although that was a current concern. The real reason was that *anyone* who drove themselves to the Houston destination and tried to park in the multitude of parking garages and assigned lots needed a treasure map and breadcrumbs to figure out where they were going and then how to get back to their car.

The Texas Medical Center, or TMC, is the largest medical complex in the world and is housed on hundreds of acres located south of downtown Houston. With thirteen hospitals, medical colleges, and colleges for nursing, dentistry, and optometry, it serves millions of patients and students each year in its world-renowned facilities. The drawback is that it serves millions of people each year. With constant road construction and the need for developing and redeveloping the area, it is a challenge to get to your appointments on time without being completely frazzled and your blood pressure in the danger zone.

Of course, she was also glad that Pookie could go with her mom because then Judy could not back out of going. Pookie could be very persuasive, and she felt certain that if her mom had tried to back out, she would have already had a message from her aunt.

She called her favorite aunt and put the call on speaker as she drove back towards the GOOF. When Pookie picked up the phone, she blurted, "Hey, Sam. Everything is fine now. I dropped your mom off after we got something to eat."

Sam's palms started to sweat, and she took a deep breath. "What do you mean, *now*?"

"Well, bless your momma's heart, and I don't want to make a big deal out of it because we were in the *Medical Center* for heaven's sake, but she got turned around after her MRI, and I had to go looking for her. Now, don't get upset, I found her pretty fast."

"You found her where?"

"Well, you see, the nurses had her put on one of those tacky gowns that don't cover your ass or flatter your figure."

Sam was trying to hold it together and gritted out, "Aunt Pookie, just tell me what happened when she got lost or turned around, or whatever, *please*!"

"I'm sorry, dear, I'll get to the point. Judy was as nervous as a long-tailed cat in a room full of rocking chairs, and after the test, the nurses told her to go back to the changing area to get dressed. She must have gotten turned around because when they went to find her to bring her back to the reception area where I was waiting, she was gone. Her clothes were still in the locker room, so we knew she was walking around holding her gown together in the back, so her business wasn't on display. We found her about ten minutes later scooting down one of the hallways with her rear end against the wall."

Sam let out a breath that she didn't even realize she was holding.

"What did she say? Was she upset?"

"Oh, no, dear. Like I said, she was fine. I'm not even sure she realized we had been looking for her. She was more worried about exposing herself to the general public than being lost. The nurse took her back to get dressed, and she never said another word about it. Like I said, she was nervous, and I think she is happy that this test is behind her now." She laughed and then added, "I just crack myself up sometimes! *Behind* her, get it?"

"Yes, I caught that. Thank you for taking her, Aunt Pookie. I hate to think what would have happened to her if you hadn't been with her today."

"I'm here to help, darlin', but I am going to fess up and tell you that we didn't get a chance to look for that workbox. We got too involved in going through all the paint colors and combinations. I'm sorry."

"That's all right, Pook. I can help her look for the box and the laptop."

Sam thought about her mom getting lost at her appointment all the way home and decided that they would tackle her missing workbox in the morning. Her hands itched to reach for her day planner, and she made a mental note to reach out to Dr. Chen's office tomorrow to let them know of this latest incident and to find out when they might be getting the results from today's tests.

When she parked at the house and started walking up the front drive, she noticed a slow-moving four-door sedan creeping up the street. At first, Sam started to quicken her pace, but then she saw the familiar magnetic sign on the side of the car that said *GOOF Neighborhood Watch*. She squinted and looked at the car that was now slowing down in front of her house and the driver who was rolling down the window. Mr. Fletcher was at the wheel and waved Sam over to the car.

Sam took a breath, plastered a fake smile on her face, and walked up to the car window, where Edwin Fletcher was in his customary overalls and a plaid shirt. She kept her eyes on his face because she didn't want to see if the sides were unbuttoned for a more comfortable seat.

"Hello, Mr. Fletcher."

"Howdy, Sam. I'm just out on neighborhood patrol."

"Yes, sir, I see that. Is there something I can do for you?"

Sam was bracing herself for the list of infractions that she was sure he was about to give her on their house when he handed her a sealed envelope.

"Can you please give this to Judy? It's the acknowledgment letter for the Neighborhood Watch program and our list of volunteer opportunities for all members. I have to say, I am pleased that she is on board with joining our organization."

Sam took the extended letter, and Mr. Fletcher gave a little salute, rolled up the window, and then began to slowly creep down the street. Sam thought to herself, *I can't imagine Mom volunteering on the neighborhood watch team. Lord, help me, but she can barely keep up with herself these days. There is no way she is going to be able to patrol the area and report on garbage cans and yard offenses.*

Sam went into the house and dropped her backpack and other daily remnants on the kitchen counter. She found her mom in the den, glued to the television, eating a bowl of popcorn.

"Hey, what are you watching?"

"It's my show! I'm just waiting to see if Kyle finally gets his head out of his rear and picks that sweet Mallory, or if that snake in the grass, Cassandra, is stirring up more trouble."

"Mom, I've told you that is just brainless nonsense that is more than likely all scripted. Why do you even watch this garbage?"

"Oh Sam, let me have a little mindless entertainment. I've had a long day, and I just want to relax and not think about anything except Kyle picking the right girl to spend the rest of his life with."

Sam did an internal eye roll and smiled sweetly at her mother.

If Judy was not upset about the day's experience wandering around the Medical Center with her rear end on display in her backless gown, Sam thought she should just quietly let the incident go.

"I get it, Mom. Hey, Mr. Fletcher gave me an envelope for you, and I put it on the counter in the kitchen. He said it was the acknowledgment letter and volunteer opportunities for the Neighborhood Watch program." Sam waited for a heartbeat and then asked, "Um, are you planning on volunteering for patrol duty?"

"No, no. I just joined so that he would help me get my new house colors approved, and I think I have finally made a decision. It's going to be cute as a bug's ear! I can't wait for all the neighbors to see the finished product."

Now, Sam had to concentrate hard not to let her internal eye roll become a real external one as she produced a smile and answered, "I'm sure you're right, just cute as a bug's ear."

Sam simply could not wrap her mind around the color scheme that was about to become a reality on the house. She didn't know what colors her mom decided on, but from the sample paint colors that Sam had seen, it was going to be nothing short of shocking. The selections had to get approval first, and certainly no amount of influence that Ms. Dolly might have on Mr. Fletcher was going to get approval for any of the color combinations that were painted on the backside of the house.

"Another thing before you get back to Miles and Cassandra . . ."

"*Kyle* and Mallory, not Cassandra."

"Yes, yes, Kyle and Mallory. I talked to Leo today, and we need to find the key to your MoneyTreeCoins account. I know you and Aunt Pookie didn't have time to look for your box of things from your office, so can we look for it first thing tomorrow morning?"

"Yes, I'm afraid we got sidetracked with paint choices and combinations, and we just ran out of time before we needed to go to the Medical Center. I promise we can look for it tomorrow. Now please, *shhhhhh*. Kyle looks like he is about to decide on who he is going to propose to. He has a ring box in his hand!"

Sam did roll her eyes this time and headed to the bathroom to get ready for bed. She wasn't sure if her mother understood just how important it was that they figured out how to access her online account, and the sooner the better. It had been a long day and she decided that she was going to soak in the tub and then look at her day planner to see what she had scheduled for the rest of the week. *Good grief,* she thought, *We have to find the key to that cyber account.* And then she added, *Dear Lord, please help me. This has been just another fine day ruined by adulting and I'm not sure if I'm cut out for it on a full-time basis.*

CHAPTER 17

The next morning, Sam heard Pearl barking and opened her eyes at her usual early pre-daybreak hour. If her eyes didn't open on their own, the neighborhood pooch made sure that none of her neighbours were going to oversleep.

Sam checked her day planner and then marched into the kitchen. There she found her mom up and drinking a cup of coffee as she studied the old handwritten recipe card that she hadn't used in years when she was baking her signature pastries. She had organized an array of mixing bowls and ingredients for baking. The all-purpose flour was on the counter along with baking powder, baking soda, salt, and yeast cakes, and in the sink, there were peeled apples and cherries soaking in a bowl of water.

Sam could see that her mom had already decided on her day's activity, and she had to take a deep breath before saying, "Good morning. I thought we were going to look for that old box of stuff from your office. We really need to get access to your, um, cyber money or wallet or whatever it is called, and get the bills paid and up to date."

"Yes, yes, we can. I was just going to get the dough started before we went out in the garage to look for it,"

Judy said without looking up from the recipe card. "Hmmm, buttermilk?" she mumbled before adding, "Mrs. Rutherford down the street asked me to make a dozen kolaches to take to work for a business breakfast, and I want to take some down to Mr. Fletcher so that he will help me with getting approval for the new house paint with the GOMO."

Sam thought this was a positive start to the day, with just a minimal amount of stalling thrown in by her mom.

"Okay, I'm going to eat breakfast, and then we will go to the garage and see what we can find. I have to be at Barre Babes to teach my first class in a couple of hours, so please, no more procrastinating."

"Sam," she laughed, "I'm not procrastinating, I'm just very good at doing these unimportant, fun things that help me put off the important things that I should be doing."

Sam had to smile and said, "Fair enough. You get your dough started, and we will meet in the garage as soon as it's rising. Do you have all the correct ingredients? I thought I heard you say something about buttermilk?"

"Don't you worry, I've been making these practically all my life. I know what I am doing."

Thirty-five minutes later, Sam and Judy were out in the single car detached garage that didn't house either of their cars. Instead, it was the storage area for the yard equipment, the Santa, Mrs. Claus, and elves that were cut out of plywood and hand painted by Aunt Pookie, boxes of old books, ceramic outdoor pumpkins, and everything else that didn't fit inside a closet in the house, which was a lot. They both stood with their hands on their hips, facing what looked like a mountain of memories, odds and ends, and just plain old junk.

Sam finally rubbed her hands together and said, "We might as well get started. There are just not that many places where it could be. It's in a cardboard box, right? Was it marked or anything?"

Judy cut her eyes to Sam and harrumphed, "Seriously? It was a box. I don't recall anything else except putting it in my car on the last day that I was in the office. That was months ago, and I've slept since then, girlie."

"Okay, well, let's just get started."

Sam started in the back of the garage and started pulling some of the old stuff out under the carport to give them a little more breathing room. She was sweating in no time and turned back to pull out another load of goods when she saw her mom leaning into a box and pulling out some old, framed pictures. Sam walked over to where her mom was lovingly looking at a picture of Grammy and Peeps.

"Mom, where is that from, and what is it doing out here in the heat and weather?

"I think it's a box that I brought back from your Grammy's house years ago after she went to glory. We were clearing everything out and getting ready to put it on the market. I want to take it inside and go through some of these things."

"I think that's a great idea. Let me haul it into the kitchen, and you keep looking for the workbox."

Sam struggled to lift the decaying cardboard box that clearly had more than just pictures in it, judging by the weight. She finally got it into the house and was starting back to the garage when she heard her mom let out a whoop.

"I found the box! It's here, Sam, with all my old office junk!"

As Sam walked back to where her mom was hovering over an old banker's box, she said, "Oh, thank goodness, I was afraid it got tossed or donated. I think we should take it inside your office and go through it there where it won't feel like we are sitting in a sauna."

Judy grinned and said, "I'm going to go check on my dough, you bring the box."

Sam started to return the items that she had moved under the carport back into the garage when she realized that she had sweated through her shorts and T-shirt. She was going to need a shower before she could leave the house.

She deposited the workbox in the office, and then Sam hurried into the bathroom to rinse off and get dressed for class. She yelled over her shoulder, "Mom, why don't you look through your work stuff and see if there is anything there that might help us with your MoneyTreeCoins account? I've got to get ready for work."

A quick ten minutes later, Sam exited the bedroom, now in royal blue workout leggings and a tank top with the Bar Babes and Buns logo on the chest. She was confident enough to wear her workout attire wherever she went and got appreciative looks from men and women alike. To a certain extent, Sam tried to be a living advertisement for her commitment to fitness, and ultimately, to one day be the symbol of her own exercise studio and fitness brand.

As she rounded the corner, she was expecting to see her mom in the office going through the office box, but the deteriorating container was still closed and exactly where Sam had placed it before her shower.

She could hear pans rattling and water running coming from the kitchen intermingled with Judy and the Beatles singing *Let It Be*. She decided that she would take that song as a sign that she shouldn't ask her mom to go through the workbox alone and that, maybe, she should just let everything be until she was here to observe and supervise.

"Mom, I need to be at the studio until this afternoon. When I come home, we can go through your workbox and your box from Grammy's house. How does that sound?"

Judy was singing and kneading the dough that she had started earlier. She smiled at Sam and said, "As soon as I get these kolaches in the oven, I'll get started."

Well, crap on a cracker, Sam thought to herself, *Now she is not going to procrastinate.*

"That sounds good, but please don't throw anything away until we have a chance to see if it's trash or treasure, okay?"

"Sawyer, I think I know when something is garbage and when it's not."

Sam knew she had pushed her mom's buttons if she was calling her Sawyer and decided to drop the subject for now. The garbage wasn't getting picked up today, so if she had to, she could always secretly go through Judy's rejected items. She walked over and gave her mom a peck on the cheek, and said, "Sorry, Mom. I'm just trying to help, and we need to get you access to your MoneyTreeCoins account as soon as possible. Also, Aunt Pookie should be here later to take you for your blood work."

"Geez Louise, Sam. I can go get my bloodwork done without a driver. There's a lab just around the corner in the professional building by the hospital."

"Fair enough, but you call your sister and cancel your ride with her then, and please let me know when you get home and that everything went okay."

Judy started to say something, and Sam cut her off as she was walking towards the front door. "Not because I don't think you can't take yourself, it's because I love you."

Judy turned around and started working the dough on the floured, wooden workboard that had been her mother's and her grandmother's before her.

When Sam shut the door, she could hear her mom and Linda Rondstadt belting out that she was no good.

Sam wasn't sure how she was supposed to take that sign.

CHAPTER 18

When Sam got to the studio, she went through her usual ritual of stowing her things in the back office, checking her day planner, and reviewing the students who had signed up for her classes to see if there was going to be anyone new or a regular that required special attention. Cara was at her desk in the office, and Darby was at the front desk checking the company emails to make sure she hadn't missed anyone who needed to change a class time or other consideration and help.

Sam set up everything she needed for her class and had her mic in her hands and the background music playing for early arrivals. She wandered back to the office and asked her boss, "Did you decide on anyone for the open barre tending position? The more I think about it, I like the bilingual woman. Isn't her name Silvia Sanchez?"

Cara looked up from her computer and smiled. "I liked her as well, but I decided to go in another direction. I went with one of our current students who is interested in some part-time work. Dolly Bunosky."

Sam's eyes bugged out, and she blurted, "Dolly Bunosky! I didn't even know that she applied. Wait, are you teasing me?"

Cara calmly shook her head from side to side and waited for Sam to digest this news for a minute.

"Look, Sam, she knows many of the clients already, so she would be a familiar welcoming face at the front desk, and she is available at any time that I need her since she is currently unemployed, single, and mature. The single and mature part works well for me because she doesn't have to be home to meet a school bus or have daycare responsibilities. She also doesn't have a spouse who might not enjoy the hours that we keep at the studio. I think it's a win-win."

"Those are all good points, Cara. I was only concerned about her, um, knowledge of everything that happens with our clients and her ability to *not* share it, to put it bluntly."

"She will be instructed on our handling of confidential information and trained just like the other barre tenders and teachers. Initially, we will hire her for a three-month trial period. After that, we will re-evaluate and decide if we want to make it a permanent placement. If there is any concern at any time between now and her three-month review about her ability to professionally handle any of the company's information or our patron's business, it will be addressed at once."

Sam nodded her head and said, "I understand. I certainly didn't mean to question your decision."

"On the contrary, I'm always happy to have your input."

Sam wandered back up to the front, trying to digest this unsettling bit of news. Students were starting to come into the studio and check in, and she greeted several regulars who were busy putting on their sticky socks that were required for safety and balance reasons and putting away their shoes, keys, and purses.

She was headed back towards the sound equipment to finish getting her mic on, and the playlist was queued up for warm-ups when Darby called her over to the front desk. Leaning into Sam so that no one else could hear, she whispered, "Did you hear who the new barre tender is going to be?"

"Cara told me when I said hello to her in the office just now."

"Well, I don't want to question her decisions, but my momma would say that Ms. Dolly was in the lead when tongues were handed out," Darby quietly murmured.

"You're right, I'm not going to question Cara's decisions either, but let me give you a little tip, do *not* ask Dolly Bunosky about her personal life. She probably has more going on in the sugar shack than both of us put together."

Darby put a sly smile on her face and said, "I wouldn't be so sure about that. Nic and I are going out tomorrow night. Just the two of us. He's going to surprise me with the details."

"I hope that's a good surprise and not another bat surprise."

"Hey, the bats were fun. He brought a picnic blanket and a basket of goodies with a nice bottle of wine. I didn't get pooped on or anything when they flew over."

"Hmm, lucky you."

CHAPTER 19

Between classes, Sam went over her outline for her oral presentation for her marketing project. She was starting to feel particularly good about the tweaking that she did, and she told Darby that she was ready for her to review it before her class presentation the following week. She wanted to make sure that she hit all the important points and high-lighted the main ideas clearly and succinctly. She attached the project to an email and sent it to Darby. With that wrapped up and checked off her to-do list, Sam and Darby started the regular clean-up and shut-down routine for the studio. They both jumped when they heard someone knocking at the locked front door.

Sam walked around the corner and over to the glass entry to see Nic standing there holding a bouquet of flowers.

Sam unlocked the door and motioned for him to come inside. Wiggling her eyebrows and slyly smiling, she said, "Well, I bet those are for me."

Nic had a slow red flush creeping up his chest and neck and said, "No, I was hoping that I could give these to Darby."

Sam was pleased to see that the normally suave and smooth ladies' man was nervous about his romantic gesture to her friend.

"I'm kidding! Of course, they are for Darby. She's in the back shutting everything down. Go on down the hall to the right."

Nic disappeared down the hall, and Sam continued back to the office to get her backpack and keys when she heard Darby squeal and then say, "Well, here I thought you were all hat and no cattle, but you sure know how to make someone feel special."

Sam smiled to herself at Darby's Alabama expressions, which she thought were even more challenging to decipher than some of her Texas ones, and yelled down the hall, "Darby, I'm going to head home if you and Nic can finish locking everything up?"

"I can take it from here, Sam."

Oh, I bet you can, Sam thought to herself, and locked the door behind her. She used her car key on the Booger to open her door and threw her backpack in the passenger seat. She checked her phone again to see if her mom had followed up with the promised text after she completed her blood work. With nothing but a blank screen, Sam sent one to her letting her know that she was on the way home and would be ready to go through her workbox, and if they had time, the box from Grammy's house. When she didn't get an immediate response, she put the phone in her cupholder and started off in the direction of home.

When her stomach let out an audible growl, Sam decided to surprise her mom and stop at Whole Foods on Waugh Drive to pick up some ready-made salads, hummus, fresh olives and bruschetta for dinner. She thought that this way they could quickly eat and then tackle the boxes. She turned the Booger around and headed towards the store that originated in Austin and specialized in natural and organic foods. Their pre-made selection was excellent, and Sam made it a habit to rely on them when she had the time and available money instead of her own cooking abilities. When she got back in the Booger and reached across the center console to place the bag with dinner on the passenger seat, she glanced down at her phone that was still sitting in the cupholder and now had several text messages waiting to be read.

Sam saw that Darby had sent three texts, and she couldn't quite work out if she was excited or upset about something. She started reading from the bottom and the first message that was sent.

Are you busy?

Did you go home, or do you have other plans?

I need to talk to you!!

Sam called Darby back and only got her voicemail, so she sent back a quick text.

Sorry. Left my phone in the car. Should be home in about fifteen minutes. Come over or call me back.

She worried all the way home about what could possibly be wrong. If it were something with the studio or work-related, she felt certain that Darby would have reached out to Cara, so this had to be personal. What Sam could not tell from the texts was if Darby happily needed to talk and share with a friend or sadly needed to talk and share with a friend. Sam hoped it was the former, and if Nic had anything to do with making her upset, he was not going to be thrilled when she got ahold of him.

She parked in her usual spot in front of the house and checked her mirrors to make sure there was not a GOOF Neighborhood Watch car coming up the street. She didn't know what she would say to Mr. Fletcher if he asked her about his lady love working at her studio. *Again, ewwwww*, she thought to herself. *How was she going to make this work?*

Grabbing her backpack, phone, and bagged dinner, she practically sprinted to the house. She could hear music playing as she unlocked the door and let herself into the brightly lit den.

"Hey, Mom! I'm home, and I stopped and picked up some salads and that hummus that you love from Whole Foods."

Judy peeked her head out of the tiny office and said, "That sounds good. I'll be right there."

Sam put her backpack, keys, and phone down on the front entry table and headed to the kitchen to unpack their dinner. Strewn across the countertops were rows of kolaches just waiting to be boxed up so that Judy could make her deliveries and freeze the remaining.

Sam couldn't help herself as she reached for a sweet-smelling cherry kolache and took in a mouthful of the pastry. Before she could even swallow, she realized that there was something different about the dough and the taste. It wasn't that they were terrible, they just didn't have that extra special flavor and texture that her mom's baking was famous for. Looking around the kitchen with her trained eye at the rows of kolaches, she now noticed that their appearance was slightly different as well.

Well, I'll be go to hell, she thought to herself, *Something's not quite right here.*

Quickly depositing the remaining pastry into the garbage can, Sam started to unbox the salads and hummus. She took some bowls out of the cupboard, opened a box of crackers, and placed everything on the small kitchen table.

Judy rounded the corner in her favorite white Huipile muumuu embroidered with multicolored flowers and vines, and her shoulder-length, rootsy blonde hair was tied back from her face with a bright turquoise bandana.

"What a pleasant surprise! I haven't had a chance to even think about dinner because I have been going through the office box and the box from Grammy's house all day."

Sam did an inner cringe and asked, "So how did your bloodwork appointment go? You were supposed to let me know when you were finished, and I never got a text."

Judy, who had been reaching for a bowl, started to move more slowly and got an odd look on her face. She cleared her throat, looked over Sam's right shoulder instead of in her eyes, and said in a higher-pitched voice, "I decided to do that tomorrow. I was so busy with my baking and then going through the boxes and all."

Sam took a couple of deep breaths and then, as calmly as she could, asked, "So, I guess you called Aunt Pookie this morning and canceled with her, and then you decided not to go? Or did it, um, slip your mind?"

"Well, your aunt was being her usual pushy self, and I came right out and told her that this wasn't my first rodeo, and I could surely get myself to the lab around the corner and get my bloodwork taken care of!"

"But you didn't, *cowgirl*, and we really need to get that done. I'm going to make you an appointment for the first available time tomorrow, and I will personally take you. No more putting this off."

Judy's eyes started to get a little watery, and she sniffed. "I'm sorry. You're right, after I had that little come to Jesus with Pookie, it did completely slip my mind." She perked up in her seat, smiled, and then added, "But you're going to be so happy with what I found and accomplished today!"

Sam figured that there was no point in making her mom feel any worse than she already did about not getting the bloodwork taken care of, so she quickly looked around and changed the subject.

"Well, I see you got your baking done," Sam said, nodding her head towards the counter filled with kolaches and trying to sound casual, "but did you change something in the recipe?"

Judy's head jerked up from where she was about to take a bite of salad, and said, "Why do you say that?"

"Um, I'm sure it's no big deal, but they don't taste exactly like your regular batches. And look at them, is it just me, or are they not as fluffy and smooth as they usually are?"

Judy's head was swiveling across all the kolaches lined up on the counters, and she silently pushed back from the table. With her hands on her hips, she continued to scan her work and then reached for a cherry-topped kolache. Taking a bite and chewing slowly, Judy turned towards Sam while still holding the offending pastry in her hand.

"These do not taste like my kolaches. Sam, what happened?" Judy whimpered.

Sam could tell her mom was starting to slide into panic mode and quickly walked over to where Judy was standing with a blank look on her face. "It's okay, Mom. I saw you had Grammy's recipe card out this morning. Did you change something?"

"No! I followed it exactly. I even went out and got the buttermilk that it called for, which I swear I never used before! Oh Sam, I really am losing my mind."

Judy sat back in the kitchen chair and shut her eyes. Little tears were leaking from the corners and slowly running down her cheeks. Sam knew from the online research that she had done on dementia that the most important thing to consider was how her mom was feeling now, in the present moment. Not to question her about the wrong ingredients or inaccurate measurements that she must have used on the subpar batch of kolaches. She sincerely hoped that Alzheimer's or some other form of dementia was not what was happening to her mother, but kindness and making her mom feel safe were the most important things she could do for her until they got some answers. Since her research had also enlightened her that dementia, or Alzheimer's, can prevent the brain from learning new tasks and information, she was feeling hopeful. The way Sam figured it, her mother's recipe for making her kolaches had to be a long-term memory. Because she had baked them for years, this was not something new that she was trying to learn and couldn't grasp. Sam was willing to hang onto any bit of hope, even if it was her own twisted analysis.

Sam reached over, took her mother's hand, and handed her a napkin with her other one. "Mom, it's going to be okay. I'm here for you, Aunt Pookie is here for you, and the rest of your sisters are here for you, and we are going to get this figured out."

As Judy was wiping her eyes, the doorbell rang, and Sam thought to herself, *Well, God bless America, now what?*

"Hold on, Mom. Let me see who's at the door," Sam said as she hustled to the front door and opened it before she even asked who was there so that she could quickly tell whoever it was that they were busy or didn't need to buy anything.

Standing in the glare of the front porch light was Darby. She was looking down at her tennis shoes and hiccupping from crying. Sam took one look at her, pulled her into the house, and wrapped her in a hug. "Oh, honey, are you okay? Come into the kitchen and tell Mom and me what happened. Maybe it will take her *mind* off her own problems."

I'm a regular comedian, Sam thought to herself.

Darby looked up at that comment and sniffed as she asked, "Is something wrong with Judy?"

Sam whispered, "We can cover that topic later over a glass of wine. Maybe a bottle."

Both women walked into the kitchen where Judy was stacking all the kolaches onto a large baking sheet, and Sam said, "Mom, Darby's here."

Judy brushed her hands off on a kitchen towel and then walked over to Darby to hug her. Pushing back and looking at Darby's face, she commented, "Hello, sweetie. It looks like you've had about as good a day as I have. You sit down and tell me what is going on in your life."

Darby plopped down in one of the kitchen chairs, and Judy busied herself with a plate and silverware for their guest while Sam was getting her a glass of sweet tea.

When they all reconvened around the table and Judy had divvied up the salad between the plates, Darby took a deep breath and started her sad story of Nic and his presentation of flowers at the barre studio.

"You know, I should have known that he was up to something when he just randomly showed up at the shop with flowers. I'm so dumb. I thought he was just being nice and that we had made a connection. But *nooo*. I guess I have learned my lesson, and I now know that if his lips are moving, then he must be lying."

"Wait, wait, wait," Judy said. "Who are you talking about?"

"I'm sorry, Ms. Judy," Darby said, "Do you remember us talking about that hunky, good-looking guy, Nic, that Sam and I met several months ago at a rooftop bar downtown?"

Sam cut her eyes quickly to her mom to see how she was taking this innocent question and the use of the word remember from Darby and was relieved when her mom nodded her head yes. Sam wasn't sure if that was just a noncommittal go-ahead with your story nod, or an affirmative, I remember head nod. Since she didn't seem upset about being asked if her memory was working, Sam decided that she would see how this played out.

"Go on, Darby. I think I know who you are talking about," Judy urged.

"So, he showed up at the studio this evening when Sam and I were shutting everything down with a beautiful bouquet. I hate to admit how easily I was impressed when he was standing there so handsome with this lovely surprise. Anyway, after Sam left, he started to tell me that he was going to have to cancel our date this weekend. When I asked him why, he said that he had a party that he had forgotten about with his gaming and computer classmates. So, you know me, open my mouth, and insert my big foot. I said, 'Don't worry about that. We can go there for our date!' Well, he kinda' stammered around and then came right out and said I wasn't invited, and that it was strictly for his fellow computer geeks. I really think he already has another date for the party that he forgot about. How can he just suddenly remember this party? I feel like such an idiot."

As Darby ended her account of the flower presentation, she let out a little moan and squeezed her eyes tightly shut. Sam and her mom looked at each other and then both grabbed one of Darby's hands. Judy patted her hand and said, "Honey, now first of all, I'm going to tell you what I have always told Sam, and that is that no man is worth a hill of beans if you can't depend on him, and the only way that you are going to change him is if he wears a diaper." Her voice got a little quieter, and she continued with, "But I am also going to tell you that I have a little sympathy with him about the memory thing. Maybe it did slip his mind. I'm having a challenging time remembering some things myself. Why just look at these kolaches that I've made for years, and I've ruined them because, for the life of me, I can't remember what I changed from the recipe card my mother gave me years ago."

Sam was taking this all in and wanted to cry herself because the woman who was talking to Darby suddenly sounded like her old mom. A woman who is confident, smart, and has a sense of humor. She was also happy that her mom was freely talking about not remembering things and that she was ready to admit that something was going on with her mind.

Darby was looking at the pile of kolaches and said, "Ms. Judy, if those kolaches taste half as good as it smells in here, I'm thinking that they are just fine. I'll be happy to test one or five of them for you."

All the women started to smile at this last comment, and Darby and Judy both felt relieved, while all Sam could think about was what method she was going to use to castrate Nic.

CHAPTER 20

When the salads were gone, the tea glasses were empty, and the remaining hummus and crackers were covered and stored, all three women walked into the living room feeling much better from the company as well as the food. Pushed to the side was the disintegrating box that Sam had brought in earlier from Grammy and Peeps' house. Stacked on and around the coffee table were framed pictures, a small photo album, and books. There was also a pile of old kitchen gadgets, including a rolling pin, a rusty whisk, and some old ceramic mixing bowls.

Sam reached for the photo album and sat on the couch where Darby joined her, and they flipped through the delicate pages with old, fading Polaroid pictures attached to the sheet with aging corner anchors. "Mom, is this you with your sisters?"

Darby pointed at the picture and smiled as she found Pookie. "I don't know your other sisters, Ms. Judy, but if they are anything like Aunt Pookie, you have an awesome family."

Everyone who knew Sam's aunt was drawn to her non-judgmental and broad-minded outlook on life, and people felt comfortable and accepted in her loud presence. Her mother's other two sisters had been involved in her child-hood, but Aunt Pookie had always been a fun and present figure as she was growing up. It helped that Aunt Pookie lived close to their home in the Timbergrove area, so she had attended all of Sam's school functions and swim meets when she was a young girl. She volunteered at the elementary school and chaperoned at her high school prom. Sam's aunt was an important figure and role model in her life and stepped in on numerous occasions when her mother could not be available.

Judy leaned over Darby's shoulder and said, "Yes, it most certainly is. That's back when families plotted their vacations on a paper map from the gas station, and you took a cooler with snacks and drinks so that you didn't have to stop unless there was a unanimous vote to take a restroom break. That looks like the time we took a trip to Dallas to the state fair in the family station wagon. All six of us were in that car—my three sisters and your grandparents." She paused for a minute and then continued with, "I remember we got to see Led Zeppelin play, and that English band introduced your aunties and me to some great rock music. Those were some good times."

Sam thought she heard some sadness slipping back into her mom's voice, but when she looked back at her, Judy had already started towards her little office. "Sam and Darby, come in here and let me show you the real treasure that I found today."

Sam and Darby looked at each other with raised, questioning eyebrows and silently communicated to each other that they had better do as they were told. When they got to the small office, they could see that Judy had also unpacked her workbox. There was a neat pile of dog-eared manila folders, an ancient Rolodex that was stuffed with business cards as well as the specialty-shaped index cards with contact information written on them, a couple of old framed photos from Sam's high school days, and a few of the Rolodex cards that were blank in a stack set to the side. The grand prize, though, was sitting in the center of her desk and was an older model laptop.

Sam's eyes lit up, and she did a little happy dance before saying, "Mom, this is great! Are you saying that this old company laptop has all your information to access your MoneyTreeCoins account?"

Judy pursed her lips and started opening the laptop. "I'm hoping so, but I can't get the dang thing to finish the startup process. See, what happens when I push the power button? It just goes through this little reboot sequence before it gives me an error message. I never had to do anything to this computer because the IT gal, Vickie, oversaw all the software upgrades and whatnot for the entire office."

Sam, Darby, and Judy stared at the laptop until, sure enough, the error message appeared, and then Darby said, "I don't know what you are talking about having a money tree and all, but I bet I know someone who could fix that computer."

Sam whipped her head around to Darby and squinted her eyes. "You're not talking about that snake in the grass, Nic, are you? The one that we were just talking about and crying over not twenty minutes ago in the kitchen, remember?"

"I know Sam, I'm not happy with him either, but I bet if *you* ask him to look at this laptop, he would be able to help you, or if he can't, he could give you the name of someone who could. I'm just saying, if you want to see your money tree on this old laptop, you should start with him."

Sam crossed her arms and tapped her foot on the ground as she looked up at the ceiling. She really didn't want to ask Nic to do anything for her at all, but at the same time, they were running out of time to try and access the cyber account before more late notices and warnings showed up at the house, or worse. Even now, the offending pile on Judy's desk was growing and needed to be addressed.

"I'm going to text him tonight and see if he can look at this laptop tomorrow, but he'd better be very worried about the little talk that we are going to have about his manners."

Darby started to chuckle and said, "Well, if it makes you feel any better, I had some pretty bad manners myself when I chased him out of the studio, flinging the flowers the whole way."

Judy added, "And Sam, it will also make you feel better to know that I did do something right today. I filled out the application for approval of the paint color selections for GOMO and walked it down to Mr. Fletcher's house. He wasn't home, but I left it on his little table by the front door."

Sam wasn't sure why her mom thought that would make her feel better, because she was sure that her mom was going to be the one who was going to be upset when the crazy colors, whatever they were, got rejected. Sam glanced at one of the piles on the desk. The collection looked to include all the paint sample cards and paint chips, along with the purchase receipts for the test paints and lists of color combinations that her mom had been working with for weeks now.

"If you're happy with the paint selections, Mom, I'm happy, and I am going to see if Nic can help us with this computer. But only because we are really in a time crunch here."

Judy nodded in agreement and added, "Grammy would say that we are off like a herd of turtles, and I hope Nic can help us with this old thing."

CHAPTER 21

Sam was up early the next morning and at the studio to teach the Rise and Behind class. She had sent Nic a text after Darby had left the house the night before asking if he could call or text her as soon as possible. She had yet to get a response from the weasel.

Sam was about to check the schedule to see who was supposed to barre tend when the front door opened, and Dolly walked in waving goodbye to her ride. As Sam looked out the glass front of the shop, she saw Mr. Fletcher's sedan with the neighborhood watch decal on the passenger side door leaving the parking lot.

Sam did an internal wince and then plastered a smile on her face. Dolly was outfitted in hot pink, leopard print leggings along with a black tank top that she had knotted on one side at her hip. Today's ensemble included a head-band with little cat ears and an armful of matching bangle bracelets.

Heaven help me, Sam thought to herself. *If I see a tail when she turns around, I won't be able to hold it together.*

Dolly had made it to the front desk and swung her large tote bag over her shoulder. "Sam, I'm so excited about working here. Now, I've gone through some basic training with Cara, but please be patient with me while I get this computer stuff figured out. I'm a whiz at online solitaire, so I figure I should catch on to this pretty quickly."

Sam suppressed a smile and said, "I'm sure you will catch on quickly, Ms. Bunosky. Welcome to the Bar Babes team."

"Oh, Sam, now that we are co-workers, I want you to call me Dolly, and listen, if you ever need a ride to work or help with a class, I am at your disposal."

"That is so nice of you, Ms. Bun . . . um, Dolly. I'll keep that in mind. I'm going to just finish getting the studio setup, and if you need any help when the clients start arriving, just yell for me."

With that, Sam made a quick stop in the office and checked her day planner and her phone. There was still no response from Nic, but it was early, and there was no telling what the gigolo had been doing last night. Sam quickly went online and made her mother an appointment for her bloodwork later that morning, and then hurried to the studio to get the music started and the equipment for the day's class arranged.

This class was almost always at capacity since many of the patrons quickly headed home to get ready for a full workday in the office or to get little ones ready for school, or both. Sam finished her set-up process and then went to the reception area to see how Dolly was managing the small crowd. Many of the women were busy removing their tennis shoes and putting on their sticky socks, and Dolly was at the computer slowly and methodically going through her check-in notes with a couple of regulars.

Sam greeted everyone and then went around the front desk to see if she could help speed up the check in process since class was starting soon.

"Dolly, do you need me? Can I help you with anything?"

"Thank you, Sam, but I think I'll be fine. I'll send anyone in who I haven't taken care of so that they don't miss any of their session, and I'll work on getting everyone else registered during class. I already have Diana Sacco, Martha Jane Blome, and Amanda Garcia on my list to add to this group. Everyone else, I believe, is already checked in."

Sam nodded and looked down at Dolly's notes, and then smiled to herself when she saw that Dolly had written down her list of names on a to-do list in a day planner. She laughed to herself and thought that Cara was right and that Dolly may work out to be the ideal addition at Bar Babes. Anyone who used a day planner couldn't be all that bad.

When class was over and Sam had gone through the process again of wiping down the rubber bands and mats, she left the studio and found Dolly wiping down the small cubicles where everyone stored their things during class. Her bangle bracelets were clanging as she sprayed and wiped each one, and her little cat ears were bouncing as she moved.

"Dolly, do you need me for anything before I head out of here to pick up Judy for a quick appointment? I have to be back to teach the noon Lunch Crush class."

Dolly stopped her wiping and said, "Is there anything I can do before you get back, and is your mom all right?"

Sam could have bitten her tongue off for mentioning her mom at all and said, "I think everything will be fine, and the next instructor will be here at any moment to get the studio set up for her class."

"Okay, Sam, I am scheduled to work until two or so, and then Darby should be here to relieve me."

"Great, I'll be back soon."

The Booger was pushing the speed limit and reminding Sam of her transgressions as the Jeep was squeaking and rattling while Sam flew over the speed bumps on her street. When she got to the house, she whipped into the circle driveway and left the Booger running as she ran to the front door. Leaning inside, she said, "Mom, let's go get your bloodwork done before I need to be back at the studio!"

Sam didn't get a response, so she stepped into the house, jogged into the kitchen, and then backtracked to the bedrooms and the office where she still couldn't find her mom. She was starting to panic when she glanced into the backyard and saw her mom sprinkling fertilizer around her fruit trees. Sam opened the backdoor and said, "Hey, Mom! Let's go get your bloodwork done!"

Judy turned and said, "Oh, hi, dear. You don't have to do this. I can take myself."

Sam was gearing up for a response and a reminder about how that had worked out the previous day when her mom said, "But before you get a mad-on, I'm just going to come with you and quietly get this done."

"Great, I'll be in the car."

Sam quickly walked back out the front door and to the idling old SUV. She could have kicked herself for leaving her cell phone in the car because she saw that she had missed Nic's phone call as well as one from Mr. Fletcher while she was searching for Judy. She hit Nic's number to call him back without checking for any messages.

Nic answered on the first ring and started speaking before Sam could even figure out what exactly she was going to say to him. "Sam, I know you are mad at me about Darby and this class party situation, but I can explain. Please at least listen to my side."

"Yeah, yeah, Nic, tell it to the judge. I'll get to your lack of tact and manners soon, but I'm afraid I have to ask for your help right now. I don't want to, but I don't know who else to ask."

Sam thought she heard a little relief in Nic's voice when he said, "Sure, anything. What's the problem?"

Sam quickly told him about her mom's old work laptop and the error message that she kept getting when she tried to turn it on. She decided she didn't need to go into detail about why they needed the computer, only that they needed it to work. He was bending over backward to be cooperative and told Sam that he would stop by their house later in the day and pick up the computer and look at it.

By the time Judy made it to the Booger, Sam was feeling hopeful that progress was going to be made on all the items on her to-do list for the day. Rise and Behind class taught, check. Mom's blood work completed, check. Old laptop in line to be fixed, check.

Thirty minutes later, Sam was already headed back home with her mom to drop her off. When they pulled up to the house, Aunt Pookie's treasured white Mini Cooper with long, plastic eyelashes on the headlights was in the driveway. Pookie was standing at the front door dressed in black leggings and a *Flashdance*-styled off-the-shoulder

T-shirt with a straw fedora hat that covered her signature hair and red-rimmed, heart-shaped sunglasses.

As Sam and Judy opened their doors, Pookie waved at them. "Hi girls, I came by to see how everything was going and to see how the blood work went yesterday."

Judy whipped her head around and gave Sam the stink eye, which she knew meant that Sam was to keep her mouth shut about missing yesterday's appointment.

"Hi, Aunt Pookie! I'm glad we caught you. I have to run back to the studio to teach the noon class, and then I will be back here to pick up Mom for her EEG appointment this afternoon."

"Darlin', I can do that for you! I'm sure you have a hundred other things that you could be doing."

By this time, Judy had made it to the front door with Pookie and said to both of them, "Ladies, in case you have forgotten, I can hear you, and it's very rude for you to be planning my day's activities and my transportation like I'm not even here."

Pookie looked at Judy and cocked her head to the side. "Sister, if we didn't love you, we wouldn't care how you were able to get to these appointments, but fortunately for you, a loving bevy of beautiful and smart women surrounds you. Now, let's let Sam get back to her busy life. By the way, a little silver fox in overalls stopped by when I was getting out of my car earlier. He was in a neighborhood patrol car, and I think he wanted to make sure I wasn't robbing the place. Anyway, I didn't catch his name and he finally said that he was looking for either one of you."

Ewwww, ewwww, ewwwww! What was it with these older women and Mr. Fletcher? Sam shuddered to herself.

"Mom, if it's all right with you, I'm going to take Pookie up on that offer to go with you to get your EEG. I have a few things that I would love to get done, and that would help me out tremendously. But only if that's okay with you, *and* you promise me that you are really going to the appointment," Sam said, trying to catch her mother looking at her to give her back her own version of a stink eye.

Judy looked calmer and said, "Of course, that's okay with me."

Sam added, "I'll text both of you the information for the appointment, and Nic will be coming by later today to pick up that old laptop. If you need to leave before he gets here, just put it in a bag and leave it at the front door."

They all agreed, and Sam got back in the Booger to return to the studio. She was feeling a lot less stressed about the rest of her day, but she couldn't help but think about the millions of caregivers who dealt with their loved ones who had dementia day in and day out. Judy wasn't even diagnosed with a form of dementia yet, and she was struggling to keep up with her daily needs and safety while still trying to perform her job and manage her schoolwork. There was no way they could afford to pay for help at this point. Heck, they couldn't pay the utilities and mortgage right now. Sam made a mental note to check out what public services were available to her mom if she was diagnosed with dementia, and to reach out to her other aunts just to let the family know what was happening in their sister's life. Sam was sure that Aunt Pookie had already looped them into the situation along with the particulars, but she owed them a personal phone call as well.

Aunt Tae-Tae and Aunt Crackers were the two youngest of the four sisters. Even though they didn't live in the Houston area, they were all still in Texas and were as feisty and fun-loving as Aunt Pookie. All the sisters were close to each other, and Sam wondered just how many private conversations the three must have had about the quietest and least outgoing in the family, her mother, and her memory issues.

By the time Sam got back to the studio, her stress level had ratcheted back up to the red zone just thinking about everything that she was possibly facing. Sam parked in the back where the employees were supposed to park and let herself in the rear door that went directly into the office. The smell of warm vanilla greeted her, and it confused her as to where it was coming from. She stowed her backpack on a hook because the visitor chairs that were normally in front of the desk were missing and went into the lobby area. The studio had never looked and smelled so good. Dolly had a candle burning on the counter and a little vase with some daisies in it next to the computer. All the paperwork was neatly stacked, and brochures and business cards were fanned out in an attractive array on the countertop. In addition, Dolly had pulled the two small chairs from the back office and angled them next to the reception desk with a little potted plant between them.

Dolly was standing behind the desk and jumped a little when Sam walked in from the office.

"Oh dear, I have got to remember that there is an entry in the back as well. You scared the bejeesus out of me! And by the way, you just missed Cara."

"Dolly, the studio looks good and smells good. Very nice touch."

"It's nothing. I just like to be busy. And useful!"

"Well, busy or not, it looks great. I have a little bit of time before my next class, so I'm going to check my emails and my planner to see what else I need to do today."

"That's good. I always say an organized day is a productive day."

Oh, Lawdy, that really is going to be me in forty years, Sam thought to herself.

CHAPTER 22

Sam spent the time she had before class started to review the notes that Darby had sent her back on her marketing project. Sam thought the comments and suggestions her friend made were thoughtful and made some good points to consider and use to tweak her oral presentation. With only one week left of class before she presented her project, Sam finally felt like she had a presentation that she was proud of and excited to give.

Toying with the idea for a few minutes, she grabbed her phone and sent off two quick texts before she could change her mind. The first one she sent to Nic.

> **The laptop is at the front door if no one is home. I'll be on campus this evening if you want to meet and talk about your bad behavior.**

The second one she sent to Leo.

> **I have my class tonight but a free afternoon. If you are available, I could treat you to the early dinner that I owe you.**

At the end of Leo's text, Sam added the kissy face emoji, hoping that he would read between the lines.

Sam grabbed her day planner and marked off her mom's EEG appointment and her marketing project that she was now ready to present to the class. This day was going well, and she was practically feeling smug that she was able to check these things off her to-do list. Sam considered briefly trying to call Mr. Fletcher back to see what GOMO infringement they had committed now, but she decided she was not going to ruin the good day vibes that she currently had and was thoroughly enjoying.

When Sam's noon class was over, Dolly came in and helped her finish wiping the mats and balls that they had been using.

"Dolly, thank you so much, but you don't have to help me do this."

"It's fine. I'm all caught up in the front, and I'm just waiting for Darby to come in and relieve me."

"Well, I appreciate your help."

Dolly turned and started to say something, then stopped herself before finally blurting out, "Sam, is everything okay at your house? Edwin and I were, um, talking about, um, its façade, and we were going to see if there was anything we could do to lend a hand."

Sam's face started to redden, and she was embarrassed that anyone was asking, much less Dolly, about the appearance and upkeep of their little home. She also thought to herself that this was why Mr. Fletcher was trying to contact her. "No, it's fine. You know Mom is working on getting the new house paint approved, and then we are going to get everything looking as good as new."

Just as the day was going so well, Sam was reminded that she still had several big problems, including fixing up their beloved home. She hoped that Dolly would relay that message to Edwin, and at least she wouldn't have to have the same embarrassing conversation with him.

Sam practically ran to the office and gathered her things before sticking her head out of the office door, telling Dolly that she was heading out for the rest of the afternoon, and thanking her for her help. She got into the Booger and checked her phone for messages. There was a text from Nic confirming that he had already picked up the laptop and was going to look at it right away. He also let her know that he would text her when he got to campus later that evening and that he would like to talk to her about Darby.

There was a text from Leo that was only a yes and the same kissy-face emoji. Sam smiled and felt a little jolt of pleasure run through her chest and trickle into her stomach.

He really can read my mind, she contentedly thought to herself, and she sent him a follow-up text that confirmed the restaurant and the time she would be there.

Sam wasn't expecting any news yet from her mom and Aunt Pookie about the EEG appointment, so she decided to do something truly decadent and treat herself to a pedicure before she met up with Leo. Guilt started to creep into her psyche that she wasn't the one taking her mom to her appointment, but Sam knew her aunt would tell her to take advantage of her rare free time.

She pulled the Booger onto Studemont and headed towards her favorite local salon, Get Nailed! When Sam entered the brightly lit salon, the store owner, Vivian Phan, greeted her like it hadn't been months since she had seen Sam.

"Good to see you, Ms. Sam. Pick your color, and I'll have a chair set up for you."

Sam wandered over to the full wall of acrylic racks that held every color variation that you could possibly imagine and struggled to decide on a shade. She thought she could relate in a small way to the frustration her mother must be having to try to select the colors for the house, and Sam didn't have to have anyone's approval. She opted for a nice blue because she figured she needed to do something a little daring and off the wall in her routine, scheduled life.

Sam settled herself in her chair and let the massage feature take over from there. The nail tech that sat in front of her and worked on her shameful toes was efficient and blessedly quiet. Sam gave herself fifteen whole minutes before she couldn't help herself and pulled her shiny day planner out of her backpack. The feeling of remorse continued to grow the longer she sat in the vibrating chair and tried to play hooky from life. She flipped to the correct tab in her planner, updated a few things, and then decided to check in on her mom and Aunt Pookie.

Just checking on you two to see how the EEG is going?

Sam waited to see if she got any dancing dots indicating a replay was on its way, and then leaned her head back to further enjoy the massage. A few minutes later, she felt the phone vibrate in her hand, and she reluctantly opened one eye to see who had messaged her.

All done, but we have a little emergency. Headed to Shearlock Combs.

Sam sat up straight in her massage chair and started calling her aunt's cell phone. She wondered what could have possibly happened if they had to go to her mom's standby beauty salon in the Heights area, which was close to where Sam was now soaking her toes. When that call went straight to voicemail, Sam tried reaching her mom on her cell as well. Again, she was sent to voicemail, and Sam knew that there was no way she was going to be able to wait until her pedicure was complete to make sure her mother was all right.

Yanking the hot towel off that was covering her left foot and leg as it was positioned on the footrest and pulling her right foot out of the hands of the nail technician, Sam blurted, "I have an emergency, and we are going to have to finish later."

The timid nail technician was startled and pushed back away from the massaging pedicure chair on her rolling stool. She had the bottle of blue polish in one hand and the paintbrush in the other. There was an immediate request for what Sam assumed was help in a different language, and Vivian came flying around the corner from the front desk to see what the commotion was all about.

"Ms. Sam, is there something wrong? You want a different color?"

As Sam was locating her socks and tennis shoes, she realized that one set of toenails was nicely trimmed and had a coat of blue polish, but the other foot was unpolished and looked pathetic. She put her sock and tennis shoe back on the paintless foot and decided to try to at least preserve the paint job on the finished foot.

Sam answered Vivian as she pulled some cash out of her wallet and tried to present it as a peace offering to the nail girl, who was now cowering behind the store owner.

"No, no. What's her name?" Sam asked, motioning with her head to the girl who had been working on Sam's feet.

"Her name is Jane."

"Ok, well, Jane was doing an excellent job. I just have a family emergency, and I am going to have to come back some other time to get this pedicure. Here's the money for the service and Jane's tip. So sorry, but I have to go!"

"Let us get you a spa thong for your foot," Vivian said as she motioned to Jane.

Jane reached into the nail trolley cart and handed Vivian a yellow foam pad that, with a twist of her hands, she quickly converted into a slipper. Vivian handed the slipper to Sam. She crammed it onto her foot and went shuffling out of the shop towards the Booger as fast as her little foam slipper would allow her to.

Sam decided that instead of trying to call her mom and aunt again, she could make much better use of her time by just heading directly to Shearlock Combs. Her thought process was that perhaps she could beat them there since she was currently closer to the hair salon than where her mom and aunt were originally at the EEG appointment.

Sam tried to calm herself and not let her imagination run wild as she turned onto 19th Street and found a nose in parking space a few doors down from the salon. Rushing out of the car, she once again started hobbling down the sidewalk with one tennis shoe on and the foam slipper on the other foot. Sam pulled open the door to the beauty salon and rushed to the front desk, where she asked the unnaturally black-haired young receptionist if Judy Martin was in the back. As he was checking the computer screen to see if there was a client by that name, the door chimes tinkled, and the front door opened.

"Coming through! We need help, stat!"

Sam recognized the voice and couldn't imagine why her aunt was trying to sound like she was an ER nurse on a television hospital drama show, but when she turned around, she let out a gasp, and her hand covered her gaping mouth. Standing next to Aunt Pookie was Judy, looking like a modern-day bride of Frankenstein. She had the small metal discs from the EEG leads glued to several sites around her head, and the lead wires that were attached to the electrodes were jutting out of her hair at various angles.

"Oh, wow! What happened?" Sam asked in an awed voice.

Judy looked like she was trying not to cry as she kept running her fingers through her hair and feeling the electrodes attached to her skull, which was only making her hair stand out further around the wires.

"Sam, I have everything under control. You see, after Judy's EEG, which went just fine by the way, the nurse had a little trouble removing these wires."

Judy was still running her fingers through her scalp and screeched, "Trouble? I'd call it more than trouble when she was removing my hair along with these electrodes! There was no way I was going to sit and let her snatch me bald while she was pulling these dang things off my head, so I grabbed all the wires and pulled them out of the machine! My hair is thin enough as it is!"

Aunt Pookie confirmed this outburst by nodding her head yes and adding, "She most certainly did. She went running out of the exam room and didn't look back. I had to get our things, and I told the front desk that I'd return their wires when we got them professionally removed. It was *fine*. She was in the car waiting for me."

This little outburst had several of the salon patrons peeking around the corner, and the emo-clad receptionist was looking longingly at Judy's wired hair.

Sam stood speechless at this account, and Aunt Pookie took the lapse in response from her niece to walk over to the receptionist and calmly ask who could see Judy immediately and work on removing the electrodes delicately.

Sam tottered over, gave her mom a little sideways hug, and said, "Mom, it's going to be fine. I'm sure these can be removed without pulling out any more of your hair."

Hands still in her hair, Judy nodded and then looked down and said, "Sam, next time you go to get your toes done, you should have them do both of your feet."

CHAPTER 23

Sam was the first one to arrive at the outdoor bistro on Washington Avenue and decided after the experience she had just had with her mother and her aunt that she deserved one glass of wine. After placing her order with the waiter, Sam sat back in her chair and closed her eyes to try and calm her mind. Before she even had a chance for the zen to set in, she felt a hand on the back of her neck and a scratchy cheek rub against her smooth one.

Without opening her eyes, she said, "Don't tell my date that I think you smell nice."

Leo chuckled and said, "Ma belle, I won't tell him, but it's just common courtesy to let him know that you are about to be aggressively pursued by a nice-smelling Canadian."

Sam opened her eyes and took in the attractive man sitting across from her. She always appreciated his good looks, but what she was really attracted to was his kindness and his ability to rally around her in whatever circumstance she was currently focused on. Top all of that off with his sexy French-Canadian accent, and really, it was everything she could do not to hurtle herself at him.

When the waiter brought her a glass of wine and placed it on the table in front of her, Leo's left eyebrow cocked up questioningly. "Are we playing hooky from school tonight? It's fine with me. I just want to know what I did, or what you did, to get you to relax and enjoy life a little bit."

Sam smiled at him and answered, "You wish. I'm still going to school tonight, but after the afternoon that I just had, I think I deserve one glass of wine."

"I guess the fact that you are here and smiling means that it can't be all that bad, right?"

"Oh, depending on who you ask, it could be that bad."

Leo motioned for the waiter to bring him the same thing that Sam was having and said, "Tell me what happened."

Sam started to relay the account that led to Sam finding her mother looking like a cross between Albert Einstein and a troll doll, and when she finished the story, she saw that Leo could barely hold back a laugh.

"I guess now the story is a little funny, but really, I have got to get my mom's health and finances figured out. These last couple of weeks have been eye-opening, and unless I can figure out this MoneyTree cyber shit, I'm worried that we may need to sell Judy's house. And I won't go into great detail, but she seems, um, to be having trouble recalling things. It's just a lot going on. On top of work and finishing this marketing class, which, by the way, I should be done with after my project presentation next week, I need to get a few things off my to-do list."

"I take it that you have not had any luck locating the key to your mother's cyber sheet account?"

Sam rolled her eyes and said, "You know good and well that I said shit and not sheet, and your accent, although sexy, doesn't make me feel any better. And, no, we have not been able to find it. That's kinda part of the whole memory issue."

Leo was looking at her with those dark, deep, understanding eyes and reached for her hand. "What can I do to help you? I think you are handling a lot, and I really would like to be of some assistance."

Sam squeezed his hand and said, "You know, I think one of your famous neck rubs might just alleviate some of the stress that I am feeling, but I guess we really should eat first since this dinner was supposed to be a payback for you helping me understand what Mom's MoneyTree account means and how it's supposed to work."

Leo glanced down at the menu that was on the table and then looked up and caught the waiter's attention and said, "We will take two of the specials to go and the check, please."

Sam did an internal little happy dance and couldn't wait to show him how good the toes on her one foot looked.

CHAPTER 24

Sam arrived at the University of Houston with an internal glow and enough time to get seated and situated in class before she sent Nic a text. She let him know that she would be able to meet him and see what he could tell her about the old laptop as soon as her professor finished the night's lecture. The following week, all the students were giving their presentations, and then the only thing left for Sam to do to complete the course was to submit an online summary and critique of the class curriculum to Professor Wood.

Sam was itching to get her day planner out and add a few notes for tomorrow, but she forced herself to focus on the class and pay attention. She was assigned to be the third person to give her presentation, and she was happy that she would be giving her report sooner rather than later so that she wouldn't continue to stress about it.

The lecture felt like it went on forever, but finally, Professor Wood finished the evening class by reminding everyone that this was the final regular class period and that the class oral presentation project started the following week. She stated again that she was looking forward to hearing the reports from her students and had high expectations for all of them.

Sam gathered her things together and then reached into her backpack for her phone to send Nic another text.

Class is over. Where do you want to meet?

It didn't take but a few seconds before Sam received a reply.

I'm in the SAC. Back right corner.

Sam knew that he was referencing the Student Activities Center, and speed walked over to the building that was the hub of student life. She spotted Nic at a table with several of his techie friends staring over his shoulders at what appeared to be her mom's old work laptop.

"Hi, Nic."

Sam knew why she was upset with Nic, but she couldn't help feeling irritated by these other friends of his as well. She wondered if they were included in the infamous party that Darby was not invited to attend.

Nic flinched a little at her greeting, and the two friends standing over him looked up at Sam.

"Sam, this is Becca and Roadkill. I hope you don't mind that I asked them to look at this notebook with me. Becca is the best we have on campus at accessing and updating memory and storage drives, and she can also look at the processor and tell us if there is a problem." He motioned using his thumb over his right shoulder at Roadkill and said, "This guy is a wizard at working through corrupted file systems and deciphering error messages and other software problems."

"Hi, Becca, and, um, Roadkill. Thanks for looking at my mom's laptop. Have you been able to get it working, for lack of a more technical term?" Sam chuckled as she said this last statement.

Becca, dressed in loose-fitting blue jeans and an over-sized hoodie sweatshirt emblazoned with a picture of the campus mascot, an alligator holding some books, and Roadkill, who had on tightly fitted black pants with his hair in a nice little man bun, both just stared at her. She mused to herself, *I guess I'm not good at geek speak*.

Nic jumped in right away and tried to explain to her that it wasn't as easy as just recharging the batteries or putting in a password to get the system back up and running. He must have realized that he lost Sam in his explanation because she just stared right back at all three of them with a blank look on her face.

"Sam, I'm sorry. This is going to take a little more time than I originally thought, and I'm still holding out hope that this is not a complete system crash. If you like, I can help your mom select a new computer that would be much faster and more efficient than this one."

"Nic, Becca, Roadkill, I'm not doubting your skills or trying to hurt your feelings, but I need this computer to work. Please, you have no idea how important this could be, and I *really* need to see what is on *this* computer."

Becca and Roadkill looked at each other, and Sam wasn't sure what silent message they were geekily mind-melding to each other, but she was starting to think that this laptop might just be false hope and a dead end. It was probably something else that should go to the recycling center.

Roadkill finally muttered, "You can't hurt my feelings. I used to hold the flashlight for my dad."

Sam had to laugh at that comment and said, "Well,

anything you can do to get me into that computer will be very much appreciated."

Nic stood up, motioned for Becca and Roadkill to take over the computer, and walked around the table to Sam. "Can I talk to you in private for just one minute?"

Sam sighed and followed Nic over to an empty table and then said before Nic ever had a chance, "Look, I told you I was not going to be happy with you if you hurt Darby, and I meant it. How could you be such a jerk to lead her on and then act like you a, either don't want to be seen with her, or b, you have another date to your IT nerd party?"

Nic looked a little shocked, and his face started to redden. "I do *not* have another date, and I feel terrible that I forgot about my IT class social. It's not a party. It's a school-sponsored event for prospective students in the IT department, and they have recruited upperclassmen, like me, to be there to talk up the program. I agreed to do it months ago for extra credit in one of my classes. I tried to explain this to Darby, who I genuinely like, by the way, and she would not let me explain what happened."

Sam considered this explanation for a moment and decided that maybe she had seen some advertisements around campus and online emails for prospective students in many of the different programs offered at the university. "Well, okay, that all may be true, but that's what you get for having such a lousy reputation with women!"

"Please, Sam, can you talk to her and explain that this is all for school and that it has nothing to do with another date? It's just a school obligation that I truly forgot about . . . because I know I'm lucky Darby agreed to go out with me."

As he said this, his face fell, and Sam could tell that he was genuinely upset by the misunderstanding that he had with Darby. Maybe he did like her as much as he proclaimed to, or as her mother would say, perhaps Nic wasn't changing, but she was starting to *see* the real Nic.

"Look, you need to try and explain to her about the commitment you made to your school department. I will back you up if she asks me about it, but I'm warning you again, don't mess with my girl."

"Thanks, Sam, and we'll continue to work on this pile of . . . um, laptop. I'll keep you posted."

"No problem, and the sooner the better."

"Ditto."

CHAPTER 25

When Sam arrived back at their house, she found her mother in the small office area, sitting behind her desk with hair that had been beautifully blown out and styled.

"I see you got all your electrodes removed. How hard was that process?"

Judy swished her shoulder-length hair over one shoulder and said, "Once they got some warm water on the glue and added some conditioning oil to my whole head, they just started to slide right off. That nurse should have given me some hint that she was going to just pull those discs out without one thought as to what she was going to take with them!"

Sam agreed and said, "The good thing is that we have all your tests completed now, and we should be hearing from Dr. Chen's office soon with the results."

Judy took a deep inhale, and Sam thought she looked like a little schoolchild who had been called to the principal's office.

"Don't worry. We're going to find out what is going on in that head of yours with the beautifully styled hair."

Judy reached up and ran her fingers through her lightly curled ends and smiled. "It does look good, doesn't it? It was nice to get my hair professionally treated and pampered again."

"Yes, it does. By the way, what are you doing in here? Are you still looking for your password?"

Now Judy looked pitiful as she extended her hand to Sam that held an unsealed envelope. Sam reached for the certified letter and flipped it over to see who it was from. Even though she knew this had to be coming and had prepared herself for the possibility, Sam's knees felt weak when she saw the return address was from the National Bank of Texas, the company that held the mortgage on the cottage. Sam slid her finger under the flap and removed the official form letter that indicated that the house was about to go into foreclosure.

Sam sat down in the small side chair and began to read the letter carefully, hoping that she would find that the bank had the wrong address or mortgage holder. She zeroed in right away on the amount owed plus interest and penalties, and almost choked.

Looking up at her mom, she said, "Maybe we can make some installment payments that would delay the foreclosure until we get your cyber account figured out."

"Keep reading."

Sam continued reading the document and finally got to the specifics of when and where the entire amount was to be paid or the house would be foreclosed on and become property of the bank. The correspondence concluded with a statement in legalese bold print that said no partial payments would be accepted and only the entire amount owed would rescue the house from the forthcoming foreclosure action.

Sam and Judy just stared at each other across the desk, and Sam finally sat up and said, "Okay, I think we need to contact MoneyTreeCoins and explain the situation and ask them to let us reset the password. We can provide them with all the documentation that they could possibly need to prove that you really are *the* Judy Martin that owns that account."

"I think that's a promising idea. I'm not going to be able to sleep tonight knowing that our home is on the verge of going into foreclosure. I can't believe that this is happening!"

"I know, Mom, it's not an easy situation to deal with, but if we can just figure out how to access your online account, this problem is going to go away."

Sam's heart silently broke as she thought about the little house on Lamonte Lane and the serious possibility that it would be one of the next ones to be replaced with a newer model if she couldn't figure out a way to help her mom. Sam sincerely hoped that she could. Voicing her predictions aloud wasn't going to help the situation, and it certainly would make her mother feel worse about her memory issues.

Sam and Judy spent the next half hour logging in to Judy's cyber account on the office desktop, accessing her wallet to see if anything had changed, and then composing an email to the MoneyTreeCoins customer service department requesting that a new passkey be set up to her wallet since the old key was no longer accessible. They offered to submit a copy of her Texas driver's license and birth certificate to prove that she was, in fact, Judy Martin, as well as anything else that they needed to verify her identity. When they finished the email and proofread it several times, they both held their breath and hit the send key.

"Hopefully, we will hear from them tomorrow, and we can get the ball rolling on transferring the funds that are in your cyber wallet to your checking account," Sam said. "Then, all we have to do is get the mortgage caught up, along with this other stack of love letters that need attention, and you will not have to worry about your house and creditors anymore."

"Sam, I've been thinking about it, and I've already decided that if we do get this money over to my checking account, I'm going to pay the mortgage off. I know I will sleep easier knowing that the bank won't have the power to ever kick us out of here again."

Sam was nodding her head in agreement and said, "I think that's a great plan. Let's call it a night, and keep our fingers crossed that MoneyTreeCoins responds tomorrow and tells us that it's no problem at all to reset your key to your account."

"I'm with you, dear. I'm exhausted, and I certainly don't have the energy to call Mr. Fletcher back tonight. He left me a message taped to the front door that said for me to call him when I got a chance tonight."

Sam jumped in quickly and said, "That's okay, I already handled that for you. I spoke with Dolly at work today."

"How would Dolly know what Mr. Fletcher wanted to talk to me about?"

Sam screwed up her face and explained, "Well, you are not going to believe this, but Dolly is *dating* Mr. Fletcher."

Judy's eyes got bigger, and she said, "Are you teasing me?"

"No. No, I'm not. He's dropped her off at work several times, and I have seen her car parked in front of his house."

Judy chuckled and said, "Your Grammy always said that even a crooked pot will find a lid that fits."

"Oh, Mom, just, ewwwww!"

CHAPTER 26

Judy's follow-up appointment to go over all her test results was scheduled for late in the afternoon the following day. This was thanks to Sam calling the doctor's office the minute that they opened and begging to be worked into the schedule. With the way things were going with Judy's finances and the foreclosure notice on the house, Sam was hoping that Dr. Chen could give them some answers. Perhaps the family doctor would be able to at least enlighten them as to what she thought was going on with her mother's memory issues, and they wouldn't have to wait any longer to find out what they were dealing with. It would just alleviate some stress for both women.

Sam made sure that she had her afternoon class covered by one of the other barre instructors and was back at the house on Lamonte Lane in time to rinse off and change into a pair of well-loved jeans, an Astros T-shirt, and a pair of flip flops. Sam figured that at least one foot looked good enough to show off, and if she had time after the appointment, she could run back to the nail salon and have them paint the toes on her other foot.

Sam was waiting for her mother to finish getting ready for the doctor's visit and decided that she would check her phone again for an email response from the MoneyTreeCoins customer service department. Frustratingly, there was still nothing from the online company, but she did see that she had missed a phone call from Mr. Fletcher. *Why can't this man get the message that Mom is trying to get this house in shape, and I don't want to talk about it with him?* Sam asked herself.

Hitting the delete button on the message that he left, she yelled to her mother that they needed to leave so that they wouldn't be late. Judy came walking around the corner with a subdued look on her face.

"Let's go and get this over with. I don't think I can handle any more bad news, and I just want to come home and work in my backyard."

"Mom, this shouldn't take long, and maybe it's not as bad as you're thinking. At least our imaginations won't continue to run away from us, and Dr. Chen will help us get whatever treatment you need, or to the right doctor."

They loaded up in the Booger and headed towards the Katy freeway to Dr. Chen's office. Sam tuned the radio to an oldies station, hoping that the music might distract her mom and lift her spirits. As Sam was driving, her phone rang, and she glanced to see that it was Nic. Answering the call on speaker, she said, "Hi Nic, please tell me that you have some good news."

"Truthfully, Sam, I was calling to let you know that the computer is completely unsalvageable. I don't think that we can retrieve any useful information. Becca and Roadkill are still tinkering with it, but it's not looking good."

"Well, that's just great," Sam answered as she quickly glanced at her mom to see if she understood that this was probably another dead end.

"I also wanted to let you know that I have left a couple of messages for Darby, and she hasn't responded. You haven't had a chance to talk to her yet, have you?"

"No, I'm sorry. Darby wasn't on the schedule to work this morning, so I haven't seen her, but when I do, I will try to explain about the party. Thanks for trying to help with mom's laptop. I'll catch up with you soon."

"Do you want me to just recycle the computer for you? We have a program here at school where we can dispose of everything properly. We will even destroy what's left of the hard drive to make sure that no one can access any of your personal information."

"Hmmm, I guess that would be the right thing to do, and it's not like it's of any use to us."

As they ended the call, Sam stole another glance at her mom, who was staring stoically out the front window.

"Sam, that sounded like your friend is not going to be able to get my laptop running again."

"No, your laptop is not going to be much help with your MoneyTree account."

There were a few seconds of silence and then Sam asked, "Mom, when you went through your box from work, there was nothing that hinted at anything about the account or the password? Maybe you overlooked something."

Judy whipped her head towards her daughter and said, "I went through every piece of paper and file that I had and sorted everything out. You saw the piles on my desk. I didn't throw anything away!"

"Don't get upset about it now, Mom. Let's get through this appointment, and then we can go home and look again."

Sam and Judy arrived at the office building that included several other clinicians and specialty practices, signed in at the front desk, and then had a seat in the waiting room. Sam checked her phone again to see if they had received a response from the cyber company's customer service and was disappointed that she still had nothing in her inbox. She told herself that the lack of response was a good sign and that they were eagerly working to reset her mom's lost key to her wallet before they contacted her with a response.

The waiting room was full, and it took a while before nurse Cathy finally opened the door to the waiting room and called Judy's name. She led both Sam and Judy down the hall to Dr. Chen's office, told them to make themselves comfortable, and that the doctor would be with them shortly. Judy fidgeted with the hem of her dress, and Sam's unpainted toes were nervously tapping as they waited for the doctor to join them in her office.

Dr. Hayley Chen gracefully entered the small room and walked around to the side of the desk, holding a small computer in her hands. Wearing an elegant designer pink silk blouse and black pants under her lab coat, Sam instantly regretted wearing her favorite holey jeans and vintage Biggio T-shirt. *One day I'm going to remember to dress like I'm going to the theater before I come to this office,* she said to herself.

"Good afternoon, ladies. Let me pull up all your test results so that I have them here in front of me before we get started."

Sam and Judy sat in silence as Dr. Chen typed away on the small laptop and then reread and reviewed the test results.

She finally looked up and smiled. "I think I have some good news for you. I want to be cautiously optimistic, but after seeing your lab results, it indicates that your thyroid is not functioning correctly. You probably both know that this gland is in your neck and that it produces hormones. Judy, your particular problem is called hypothyroidism, where not enough of the thyroid hormone is being produced."

Judy reached over and grabbed Sam's hand and said hopefully, "Are you saying that I don't have dementia or a memory problem?"

"What I'm saying is that yes, you probably have been experiencing some memory impairment and difficulty concentrating, but those symptoms should eventually resolve with a medication that I will be prescribing for you. It will also help with other symptoms like weight gain, hair loss, extreme fatigue, and a rapid heartbeat. Have you noticed any of these other symptoms, Judy?"

Judy squirmed in her chair, reached up to finger her hair, and said, "I may have put on a few pounds since I haven't been working, and I just thought my hair was thinning because I was getting older."

Sam was not a crier. In fact, she prided herself on being mentally tough, but she found that her eyes were wet, and she was smiling ear to ear. She was so happy with the diagnosis because she knew that this was something that they could manage together. Sam realized from her dementia research that they were extremely lucky that her mom's thyroid was the culprit of her forgetfulness and memory fog. Sam knew that most families didn't get this break and went on to deal with the complexities and everyday problems of taking care of a loved one with irreversible dementia. Once her mom was on medication and her thyroid hormones were back in the range they were supposed to be in, her sweet mother should be able to remember where she put her phone, her recipes, and, hopefully, the key to her account. Although Sam didn't know if they had the time to wait on medication to clear up her memory problems before the house was foreclosed on, and they were forced to find another place to live.

Dr. Chen continued, "I'll start you out on a low dose, and then in two months I'll have you do some more lab work so I can see if your numbers are heading in the right direction. It can take from four to six months before the hormone level is back where I want it to be, but we will take this one step at a time. Your other tests, the EEG and MRI of the brain, all came back normal."

Sam thought to herself, *Nope, we definitely do not have four to six months before we are on the streets with the rest of the homeless population, but I'll take this good news any time over a permanent dementia diagnosis.*

Judy said, "Dr. Chen, I think I just peed my pants with that happy news!"

All three women laughed, and Dr. Chen stood with her small laptop and said, "I'll get Cathy to bring you some literature on your condition and give you the paperwork for the lab work that you will have done in eight weeks. I have already sent your prescription to your pharmacy, so you should be good to go. Feel free to call me if you have any questions."

When they got back in the Booger, Sam checked her phone for emails, and her inbox had a new message from the customer service at MoneyTreeCoins. "Mom, we got a response from the cyber company. Should we open it now or wait until we get home in front of your computer?"

Judy sat for a few seconds and then said, "Let's soak up this good news from Dr. Chen for a bit, dear. Put some music on the radio that I can sing to."

They entered the GOOF neighborhood with Lynyrd Skynrd serenading Alabama, and Sam hoped that it was a good sign that they, too, would be going home forever to their sweet home on Lamonte Lane.

CHAPTER 27

When Sam and Judy got home, they both noticed the note taped to the glass storm door that protected the wooden front door. As Sam reached up and removed the note, she knew that she now recognized the handwriting.

Without even opening the note, Sam said, "Mr. Fletcher is being way too helpful. I don't know about you, but he's driving me nuts."

"He's just trying to be neighborly, Sam. Let me see what it says," and she took the note from Sam as she unlocked the front door.

"He just wants me to come by the house. I bet he wants to give me the paint approval forms from the HOA."

"Sure, I bet that's it," Sam commented without letting her mom see her display a healthy dose of eye-rolling with her response.

"Mom, I'm happy to handle that for you. Let me get in touch with him and see if he wants me to pick up the approval forms. Heck, I could even tell him to send them with Dolly to work. We're both on the schedule tomorrow, and he almost always drops her off at the studio."

"I guess that would be fine, but let's go read that email from MoneyTreeCoins and see what they have to say. I'm feeling good about how this day is going, and I feel like this is going to be more good news."

Sam and Judy went to the office, and Sam sat down and logged in to her email account. Judy was standing behind her so that she could read the email at the same time.

Sam positioned the arrow over the unopened envelope and took a breath, "Here we go."

The email opened, and they both silently read the letter.

Dear Ms. Martin,

We understand that sometimes there are situations where the nineteen-digit key to your account and wallet is misplaced or lost. However, while we sympathize with this unfortunate event, MoneyTreeCoins is not able to reset your key or give you access to your account without the use of the original key that you created when you initiated your account. These terms and conditions are included and agreed upon before an account can be opened with our firm. This safety protocol is for you as well as for MoneyTreeCoins.

You will be happy to know that the coins that are in your account and that can be accessed along with your original personal key will be honored perpetually, so perhaps there is still a chance that your key will be recovered, and you will be able to monetize your investment.

Thank you for investing with MoneyTreeCoins.

Sincerely,

Customer Service

MoneyTreeCoins

Both women silently digested this information for a few minutes, and Sam finally said, "Mom, we are not going to get any help from your old laptop, so I think the only thing to do is to go through the paperwork from your workbox again. At least we now know that we are looking for a password or key with nineteen digits in it. If we can't find the key now, maybe it will come back to you when your thyroid medication starts to kick in. Until then, I think we should contact the bank to see if they can give us more time to raise the money needed to bring the mortgage payments current."

"I am so sorry. I can't believe this is happening to me—to us! I just can't recall anything about a key or a password."

"Show me everything that was in your workbox, and are you sure that you didn't throw anything away?"

"No! Look, here's the stack of my personal papers, which were just some old bills and some work notes. My Rolodex just has contact information for the companies that we did business with and the state and federal agency numbers that we called when we had questions about the oil and gas reports that had to be submitted monthly to the General Land Office and the Texas Railroad Commission. The only other thing was these old pictures of you that I had on my desk."

Sam went through the personal paper stack and decided that the entire heap needed to be shredded and recycled. She thought the old pictures of her could probably be retired as well, and she even took the backs off the frames to see if there was a mystery piece of paper with a key. She grabbed the Rolodex and took her time flipping through all the cards, and she didn't see anything that screamed, I am a secret key—do not lose me! The old-fashioned circular phone book looked more imposing than it really was because half the cards were still blank, and a few of the blank cards were now being used as organizational markers on Judy's piles on her desk.

Sam looked at the small desk and decided that some of the piles were simply clutter. She asked her mom if it was okay to remove them so that she would have more room to work. They could then go through the stack of other past-due bills and items that needed their attention.

The pile of paint chips, sample cards, receipts, and Judy's handwritten notes for paint combinations for the house were all picked up and placed in a large plastic storage bag and positioned in the corner of the office floor. The personal receipts and old paperwork were also marked to be shredded and placed on the floor, along with the old, framed pictures of Sam and her mother. With the desk cleared off except for the pile of bills and account notices, Sam and Judy opened each one and sorted and prioritized them according to the amount owed and how late the payment was from the original due date.

Judy, feeling more than a little embarrassed, looked at Sam and said, "I guess it looks like I'm not going to have a pot to piss in or a window to throw it out of."

"It's not looking great, but let's get the utilities up to date. I have a little money saved up for future school classes, so I can help with those as well, and maybe we can buy some time with the bank. I'll add contacting them to my to-do list for tomorrow."

By the time they had done what they could with the utility bills and prioritized the remaining bills that needed to be paid, Sam decided they both deserved a nightcap. On the one hand, they needed to celebrate Judy's health diagnosis, and on the other hand, they both wanted to commiserate over the negative response from MoneyTreeCoins. Sam went to the kitchen and poured herself a budget-friendly glass of Sideshow cabernet, which she thought was a great name and a perfect description of her current life. She brought out Mr. Tito for her mother, who always had a bottle on hand for when she was feeling dehydrated or dispirited, or her current television bachelor was about to propose to the wrong girl.

Sam and Judy sat at the kitchen table with their drinks and started reminiscing about their house and the great memories they both had of living in the GOOF area. They laughed as they recalled the neighbor that regularly took their parrots out for a walk—cage and all—propped up in a stroller, and when Mr. Fletcher started to feed a stray cat and that cat got the Romano's pet cat pregnant, he dropped off cat food on the Romano's porch that was labeled "child support". They talked about the Lamonte Lane Christmas decorating work parties and the nights when everyone just happened to be outside. Outdoor folding chairs were brought out and assembled on a driveway, and neighbors enjoyed each other's company while the kids ran amok playing tag or hide and seek. Even though the area was changing, they truly did love their home and their neighbors. By the time they had finished rehashing their history in the house, the Sideshow wine bottle was almost empty, and Mr. Tito had Judy well hydrated.

"Iz okay, Mom. I'm gonna figure out how to stay here."

"And I'm gonna member that key!"

Sam got the giggles and said, "I think we've been over-served. We're ssshlurring a lil' bit."

Judy giggled, too, and said, "We're not shlurring, Sam, we're talkin' in cursive."

CHAPTER 28

It was raining the next morning when Sam opened one eyeball to turn off her alarm. Her slight headache and the rhythmic sound of the rain made it especially hard for her to force her eyes completely open. As was customary, Sam picked up her day planner and checked her schedule and to-do list. After committing her day's work schedule to memory, she added contacting the bank about the mortgage to her daily list of things to accomplish.

It rained a lot in Houston, and she often heard people say, "If you don't like the Houston weather, just give it fifteen minutes, and it will change." Knowing that it was a true statement, Sam prepared to leave the house wearing her rain jacket and Hunter rain boots to protect her daily workout attire, but she also grabbed her hat and sunscreen to reapply when the sun came out later and turned the Houston area into a steam bath.

Sam arrived at the studio early enough that she just knew she would be the first one there, but as she caught her first glimpse of the building, she could see that the studio lights were already on. She knew that Dolly was scheduled to work, and she said a silent prayer that she had missed the daily drop-off by Mr. Fletcher. She also felt a little guilty about thinking to herself that it was nice to have the barre tender on time and ready to go before she even got there to prep the studio for class. Darby and some of the other younger employees usually pushed the envelope on being punctual for the early morning opening. Cara seemed to be spot on when she hired the mature barre tender, but Sam still couldn't help being a little leery of sharing anything with Dolly that was happening with her personally. The neighborhood gossip mill whirled and whirled with just the slightest hint of a misstep or GOMO infraction, and she was sure there was already talk about the little old bungalow on Lamonte that was just begging for some attention along with a new coat of paint.

Sam parked the Booger behind the studio and let herself in through the back door that led to Cara's office. She quickly stowed her backpack, checked her phone for new messages, and saw that Nic had reached out and asked about Darby and said he would like to talk to her again. *Geez,* she thought. *I said I would talk to her when I saw her.* Pulling out her day planner, she added a note to talk to Darby and to send out an email to the other Bar Babes instructors to see if she could pick up any of their classes to help with their finances.

She walked into the reception area and said a quick hello to Dolly, who was standing behind the computer practicing her computer skills on the software program, Zenful, with her bedazzled cheaters on the end of her nose. The fresh flowers in a glass vase and citrus-smelling candle were a nice touch, and the reception area was clean and tidy. Sam knew that was all Dolly's undertaking.

Dolly looked over the top of her sparkling glasses and said, "You have a full class for the Rise and Behind group, and I can give you the breakdown of new students, or at least the fairly new, and your group of regulars. That's what you like to know, isn't it, dear?"

Sam was amazed at Dolly's efficiency and answered with a thank you and a little more guilt entering her heart for loving that Dolly was that perceptive.

"I'm going to prep the room. It looks like you have everything under control, and, by the way, it smells lovely in here."

"I'm here to help, Sam, and speaking of help, my offer still stands if you and your mom would like my assistance."

"I know, Dolly, that's very nice of you, but hopefully we can resolve our little hiccups with GOMO soon."

Sam glided into the studio to gracefully put an end to the direction the conversation was going and got mic'd up and the background music playing. She greeted her students who were coming in and decided to clear her mind of her current financial worries and give the ladies her undivided attention and a good, challenging class.

When the session ended, she went through her cleanup process but left her mic on since she would be running the morning Barre Stars class and then the Wishful Shrinking class that followed it. She casually let herself into the back office while the clients were gathering their belongings, and then attempted to get through to someone at the bank. Her real mission was to get the bank to agree to extend the deadline to get the mortgage current, but at the very least she needed the name of someone to present her request to.

After going through the automated process where she was handed off several times, Sam finally got a live person who was just as eager to pass her off to another person in their residential financing group. Sam was able to leave a voicemail for Mr. Charles Wilburn. She thought to herself that if that didn't sound like a stuffy banker's name, she didn't know what did, but at least she now had a name. She was trying to send positive vibes through the cell towers to Mr. Wilburn as she left her syrupy sweet message. She hoped that when he called her back, he would be indulgent and happy to work with a new payment schedule for her mom.

Sam was glad that she got in touch with someone at the bank. Even if she hadn't actually had a real conversation with anyone yet, she was on the right track. Her head was feeling clearer now that she was on her second bottle of water and the rain was letting up, so Sam took that as a positive sign for good karma for the rest of the day.

After completing the call with the bank, Sam quickly checked on Judy to make sure that she remembered to go to the pharmacy and pick up her new thyroid prescription. Sam then went back into the studio to greet the next round of incoming clients.

With the stress of her mom's health concerns from the past couple of months starting to ease up, Sam was reminded how lucky they were that the diagnosis was not a more serious and permanent, irreversible memory issue. Dr. Chen had said that it could take several months before Judy's memory concerns cleared up, and even that didn't guarantee that she would remember anything about a MoneyTreeCoins key for access to the online account that had Judy's life savings in it. With that in mind, Sam promised herself that she would do the best she could to save their home, but if they ended up having to sell it quickly to one of the circling, eager builders trying to build in the GOOF area, the equity in the home could give her mom some financial security, and she would be grateful for that outcome as well. She thought to herself, *I'll be grateful, but that doesn't mean that I have to be happy about it.*

Sam also took a moment to recognize how much she loved working with her students and leading them through their barre practices and hopefully to a healthier lifestyle. With everything that had been going on lately, she had forgotten to feel the joy and happiness that being an instructor at Barre Babes and Buns had always given her. Besides her mother's health scare and making sure she was on the correct path to recovery, Sam knew that her highest objective was to get her diploma and focus on owning and managing her own barre studio. Even if taking only a couple of classes a semester took her a lot longer to get said diploma, she knew she was on the right path. When the mortgage situation was handled and her marketing project was presented in her final class, she was going to listen to some of her Grammy's wisdom. The sweet old lady had always said to remember that life was too short not to include some laughter every day, and if you were having trouble with that, to call her, and she would laugh *at* you. She wasn't around anymore to add laughter to Sam's day, but just thinking about her made Sawyer Anne Martin smile.

CHAPTER 29

Sam finished off the day by meeting Darby for a quick drink at one of their favorite restaurants. She had finally reached her friend by text message, and they agreed to meet at B.B. Lemon on Washington Avenue. When Sam arrived, Darby was already set up at a bartop table in the outdoor section of the restaurant that was shaded under a huge white permanent tent. She gave Darby a hug, placed her backpack on the extra chair, and scanned the barcode on the table to bring up the cocktail and dinner menu.

When the waiter came by, they both ordered the watermelon salad with grilled salmon and a glass of pinot grigio. It seemed to both women that they needed a girl's night out to catch up on what was happening in each of their lives and talk about topics other than work and school.

Sam started with, "So, what is happening with Nic? Did he get a chance to explain about the party? Tell me everything."

Darby tucked her hair behind her ears and adjusted the aviator sunglasses on top of her head before answering. "Yes, yes, I finally talked to him earlier today. He told me all about the meet and greet that his department heads asked him to go to for prospective students. I'm just still on the fence about him *forgetting* about the event," as she made air quotes.

"Well, I, for one, am going to be a lot more forgiving and kinder to people who say they have forgotten something. Darby, I know I haven't shared all the details of what's been going on with my mom, but memory issues are real, and they don't just affect old people. Young adults in their thirties and forties can experience the early onset of dementia." With her voice rising, she continued with, "And another thing, did you know that women outnumber men two to one worldwide for experiencing dementia? Memory issues are a real and devastating thing!"

"Um, Sam, I'm sorry. I can see that you are getting worked up about this, and I know it is something that has truly touched you. Tell me about your mom and what's been going on. She was so sweet and understanding the other night when I was there crying and whining about Romeo."

Sam took a deep breath and started at the beginning with the house needing attention, past due payment notices, the lost key to the online account, her mom's memory issues, the doctor visits, and finally about her diagnosis and the prognosis for a clearing of Judy's brain fog with some time and medication.

"I don't know how much longer we will be able to stall the bank that holds the mortgage, but I have hounded Mr. Wilburn, who works there, all day. I'm hoping that he will give us some more time to get the payments current."

"Well, bless your heart. I had no idea you were going through all that. I mean, I know from my visit last week that your mom was struggling to get her old computer to work, but I didn't know you had so *much* on your plate. What can I do to help you?"

"I took your advice when you were over at the house the other night and got Nic to help me with Mom's old laptop. My thought was that if he could get it to turn on and reboot correctly, all the answers we were needing for her online account would be on that computer."

Darby cocked her head and said, "Now that you say that, Nic did say that he has something to give back to you."

"It's probably the dead laptop that I told him to get rid of. I was a little iffy with my answer about disposing of it. You can tell him to recycle it. I certainly don't need any more old junk that I will probably just have to move soon."

They both sat there for a second digesting all that was happening and sipping on their white wine when Sam asked, "When do you plan on seeing him again?"

Darby looked a little sheepish and then answered, "I told him I was having dinner with you, and he said he would wait for however long it took, but he would like to meet me for dessert at Sweet Indulgences in the Heights. He has told me repeatedly that he is sorry and that he would like to make it up to me by taking me on a surprise date this weekend. What do you think?"

"My friend, I think that if you have feelings for him, and we give him the benefit of the doubt that he forgot about his school event, you should let him take you on that surprise date. But as Aunt Pookie would say, don't be sharing the sugar with him until you're sure he feels the same way that you do."

"Darlin', I'd be happier than a tornado in a trailer park if he turns out to be the man I think he is."

"You go, girl."

CHAPTER 30

Sam still had to work on the weekend, but she wasn't scheduled to lead as many classes as she was during the regular work week. She spent the extra time that she had reviewing her marketing presentation and helping Judy go through the garage and the accumulation of rubbish from past celebrations, events, and old household items that at the time were too good to just get rid of. Years' worth of items that needed to be sorted between a donation pile, a recycle pile, and a trash pile took them several hours over both days.

Sam wondered if this was her mom's way of preparing for the inevitable or if she was hoping to find a box or a bag that contained a treasure chest that held the key to her savings account. The weekend-long project kept them both busy, and Sam considered that the process was helping her mom get her life into focus.

While Sam was at work, Judy worked on weeding the old flowerbeds and decided to revisit her kolache recipe to see if she could figure out what had gone wrong with her last batch. She was getting out all her baking paraphernalia when she glanced out of her kitchen window into the backyard. Judy thought about it for a second, and then she went out the backdoor and stood at the base of one of her lemon trees.

Very carefully, she reached up and removed several of the ripened fruit. The tree had been planted before she bought the home over twenty years ago and was now so mature that they generally had a constant supply of the tart fruit.

She knew that her thyroid medicine hadn't had a chance to positively affect her memory because Dr. Chen had said it could take months for her forgetfulness to resolve itself, but she suddenly knew what was wrong with the last batch of kolaches. Grinning and singing along with some of her beloved oldies on the radio, she planned to surprise Sam when she got home from work with a fresh plateful of their favorite pastries.

When Sam pulled up to the house after leading her last class of the weekend in tucking, pulsing, and plieing, she couldn't decide if she had the energy to do anything other than take a long relaxing soak in the tub. She was going to make herself start a load of laundry, so her workout gear was ready to go for the week ahead, and then decided she would spend the rest of the evening watching an old classic movie. Entering the front door, Sam heard her mom's typical light rock channel blaring, and the smell was nothing short of divine.

Sam deposited her backpack on the side table by the door and wandered into the kitchen. Every counter was either being used or had been used to mix and knead pastry dough or was filled with kolaches on racks waiting to cool so they could be packed and stored.

"Mom, I could smell these lovelies the minute I opened the door."

Sam nonchalantly eyed the kolaches with a practiced eye to see if they looked like they were supposed to and were not lumpy or wonky like the last batch Judy had produced.

"Sam, I figured out what I did wrong last time! I know it's way too early for my new medicine to be helping my memory, but I looked out the window earlier and saw the lemon trees. It's the lemons! When we first moved into this house, that tree was already producing lemons. I had to change my recipe one day because I didn't have any buttermilk, so I made my own. I used milk and lemon juice to create my own blend of buttermilk, and those kolaches were fabulous! I have used that secret blend ever since."

Sam could see that her mom was so pleased with herself for figuring out what had gone wrong with the last baking attempt, and Sam was tickled to see her mom in such a great mood.

"Let me see if they taste like your gold standard kolaches," Sam said, reaching for a cherry-topped pastry.

She was right. Whatever she did with the milk and lemon juice did the trick. These were her mom's celebrated kolaches that friends and neighbors raved about.

"Mom, this tastes ah-mazing."

Judy was so thrilled, and it filled Sam with joy to see pieces of her old mom coming through the fog and despair that had enveloped her for months. Even if the medication was not completely correcting her thyroid problem yet, just the relief from knowing that Judy had a treatable condition was enough to make her lighthearted and delighted. Sam remembered her promise to herself to laugh a little every day and said to her mom, "You finish up in here, and I'll start some laundry, then we can clean up and meet on the couch. Let's eat kolaches for dinner and watch a good old black-and-white movie. We can even ask Aunt Pookie if she wants to come join the fun. It'll be like old times, okay?"

"Sawyer Anne Martin, I think that is a great plan. I'll call Pookie, and you go get yourself cleaned up."

Sam grabbed her backpack and headed to the back of the house to the bedroom that she had slept in practically all her life. After sorting her clothes, she went out to the garage where the washer and dryer were to start her laundry, and then went back inside and started her bath water. She quickly checked her day planner for tomorrow's work schedule and realized that this was a big week for the Martins. She would finish her marketing class after her presentation, and between classes at work, one way or another, she was going to talk to the bank about the foreclosure notice on their home. Depending on the bank's verdict, she may have to do some research on which homebuilder was looking for a financially weakened homeowner and would be ready to swoop in and buy the bungalow. She wasn't going to force the issue any longer about the key to the MoneyTreeCoins account. Maybe, if the stars aligned, in four to six months, her mom would remember the key or where she had stored the information. It would be too late to save the house, but Sam didn't know what other options they had at this point. She added looking at possible buyers for the house to her to-do list and then decided to put everything out of her mind until tomorrow.

Letting the steam and hot water work their magic on Sam's tension and exhaustion, she felt like a limp noodle when she finally made her way back to her bedroom. Dressing in a pair of old faded pajama shorts and a skimpy tank top that had seen better days, she walked out to the garage to hang her workout gear to air dry. With her rear in the air and head buried like an ostrich in the washer to retrieve every sock and athletic bra, she heard someone clear their throat.

Sensing that this was not going to be anything short of embarrassing, Sam clutched as many of the wet items as she could to her chest to cover her skimpy, braless attire. She turned around to see Mr. Fletcher standing in his overalls with his wire glasses on top of his head. She prayed that meant that she wasn't in focus, because he certainly could get an eyeful if he could see clearly.

"Excuse me, Sam, but I have been trying to get in touch with you or Judy for several days now. Um, is there something that I can help you with inside that washer? Is something broken?"

Sam wasn't sure where to start with her response but was able to finally squeak out, "Mr. Fletcher, no, the machine is fine, and I, um, explained to Dolly, I mean Ms. Bunosky, that we are trying to get everything straightened out around here. If you can just give us a little more time, we are working on getting the house looking better and up to GOMO standards."

Before he could answer her, they heard a car door slam shut, and they both turned to see Aunt Pookie's Mini-Cooper in the driveway and her aunt exiting in her typical kitschy fashion. Spotting her niece in the garage holding a load of laundry with what appeared to be a small farmer, Aunt Pookie walked towards them.

Prepared for an evening of lounging and watching television, Pookie had thrown on a butterfly print, flowing caftan that floated behind her as she walked up the driveway. She had changed the color of her swooping bangs from magenta to dark blue, and she had earrings in her main hole that were shaped like giant ladybugs in addition to all her normal mini gold hoops that went up her ear helix.

"Hello, darlin'," Pookie said to Sam, but she was staring directly at Farmer Brown. "Do you want to introduce me to this man and tell me why you are out here in your pajamas with a load of wet clothes?"

Sam finally regained some of her composure and said, "Aunt Pookie, this is our neighbor, Mr. Fletcher. I believe you may have run into him before when he was trying to get in touch with us. He's been helping Mom get her paint selections approved with GOMO."

Mr. Fletcher switched the folded paper he was holding in his right hand to his left one and offered his now free hand to shake. "Nice to formally meet you, Pookie. Please call me Edwin."

Sam decided she had better nip whatever was happening here in the bud and said, "Mr. Fletcher, if that's all you wanted to talk to me about, I promise we are in the process of getting this place in tip-top shape."

Mr. Fletcher turned away from Aunt Pookie and said, "I'm only here because I need help understanding this form that your mom filled out and brought down to me. It's the request for approval of the new house colors that she selected. You see, you must put the name of the paint and then the exact code for the shade as specified by the manufacturer. I always go to the paint store and verify that the color is what the homeowner thinks it is. I took your mom's form to the paint shop, and I could verify the main color, but the accent color appears to have a problem."

Before Sam could say anything, Aunt Pookie said, "Well, Edwin, do come inside, and we can figure this out."

Sam wasn't entirely sure, but she thought her aunt was eyeing Mr. Fletcher like he was a funnel cake topped with powdered sugar from the Houston Livestock Show and Rodeo. *Ewww, what was it with older women and Little Boy Blue here?* she thought to herself.

Pookie sashayed and flowed in front of the group like a line leader in kindergarten, followed by Mr. Fletcher and Sam, who had continued to hold her damp clothes as a shield, towards the backdoor.

When they entered the house, Judy was in the kitchen wrapping up the batch of kolaches that were now cooled and plating some for their dinner and movie combo date. Looking a little startled to see the three entering the back-door, Judy said, "Mr. Fletcher, Pookie, what's going on?"

Of course, Pookie took the lead, guided Edwin towards the kitchen table, and offered a chair for him to sit in. "Judy, Edwin, here, has some paperwork he would like to go over with you. Maybe it would be the hospitable thing to do to get him some tea and one of those lovely smelling kolaches?"

Sam started to speak up but was cut off by Judy saying, "Edwin, please sit down and I will get you a nice fresh kolache. I'm sure that's the approval for the house paint you need to give me."

Judy then turned to Sam and said, "Dear, why don't you go do something with those wet things, and maybe change your damp shirt?"

Sam glanced down and saw that while she was clasping the wet laundry to her body, the entire front of her night-shirt and shorts were now nicely damp and leaving even less to the imagination. She backed out of the kitchen and said a silent prayer that between her mom and Pookie, Mr.

Fletcher would get the information he needed and promptly leave before he started measuring the height of their unmown lawn or inspecting where the trash cans were located on the side of the house. By and large, she thought to herself, getting paint colors approved may not even be necessary if she couldn't get the bank to extend them some time on the mortgage.

Sam changed into a pair of dry shorts and a loose T-shirt and was hanging her load of laundry strategically around her bedroom and bathroom when she heard raised voices. Shaking her head to herself and thinking that she had better check on the grownups, she eased back into the kitchen. All three were seated at the table, with Mr. Fletcher bookended with her aunt and mom on each side of him. Mr. Fletcher was pointing at the form her mom had filled out, and he said, "Judy, I promise I didn't change anything on this form. I simply took what you gave me and presented it at the paint store. There is no such color."

Sam quickly surmised that her mom had filled out the form incorrectly and now couldn't recall what the paint color data was supposed to be. "Mom, let me go get the pile of paint information that we cleared off your desk the other night, and I bet we can straighten this out quickly."

Aunt Pookie said, "Good idea, Sam. Take your time. We can just have a nice visit while we wait."

Sam wasn't about to let this drag out and miss her movie night, so she hurried into the office, where she grabbed the storage bag on the floor with the entire stack of paint colors, receipts, and notes that her mom had made and that they had placed neatly in a corner. She plopped herself down in the remaining chair that was directly across from

Mr. Fletcher and said, "Okay, I have all the paint samples and combinations that Mom was working with. Tell me which one is giving you a problem."

Mr. Fletcher flipped the GOMO form around to face Sam, and she scanned down to where Judy had listed the paint names along with the manufacturer numbers. The first color Judy listed was called Melting Sunset and she listed the manufacturer code as FP-MS995040663. The next color on the list was Sherwood Alder Tree Green, and the manufacturer code listed beside it was FP-SAM0521199411342009.

Mr. Fletcher said, as a way of explaining, "The FP stands for Felts Paint, and the next letters in the sequence are the first letters of the name of the color. You see, MS stands for Melting Sunset, so the letters for the green paint should be SATG, not S-A-M, and then there are too many numbers after the letters. There should only be nine, and Judy listed sixteen. I just need the correct code for Sherwood Alder Tree Green or the correct name of the paint for the code that starts with SAM, without the extra digits, of course."

Sam felt herself start to tremble all over, and she looked up at her mom. "Mom, where did you get the code for the paint?" They stared at each other for a minute, and then Sam and Judy both started digging through all the paint samples, receipts, and notes that Sam had pulled out of the bag.

Aunt Pookie laughed and said, "You two are acting nuttier than a five-pound fruitcake. What's going on?"

"Oh my gosh, Aunt Pookie, if this is what I think it is, all of Mom's financial troubles are going to be solved!"

Edwin looked at Sam as she said this and tilted his head questioningly. Sam caught the gesture and said, "It's a long story, Mr. Fletcher, but I hope this will stay between the four of us."

He quietly said, "I'm not one to gossip, Sam. I've only tried to keep the neighborhood standards high for all of us who live here."

Sam felt her face heating up and knew it was turning a light shade of red as she just nodded back at Mr. Fletcher.

As they continued to look through the pile, Judy suddenly pulled out the Rolodex card that she had labeled "Paint Ideas" on one side, and when she flipped it over, it said M Tree (Green)—SAM0521199411342009.

"Mom, was this card in your Rolodex?"

"Yes, it was, but when I started using the blank cards from the Rolodex to label things, I thought the green was the green that we chose for the house. I'm sorry, I've just been so confused! Do you think this is the key we've been looking for?"

Aunt Pookie slapped the tabletop and said, "There's only one way to find out. Come on!"

All four members of the kitchen group pushed their chairs back, and Pookie once again was the line leader to the small office. Judy sat down behind the desk, and Sam stood behind her as she started to log into the MoneyTreeCoins website.

Edwin and Pookie stood in the doorway, and all you could hear was Judy tapping away at the keyboard.

"Okay, Mom, this is as far as we got before. Click your wallet icon."

Judy did as she was instructed, and a box came up that asked for the user's personal identification key. Sam held the Rolodex card in her hand and started to slowly read the nineteen-digit number aloud as Judy typed the sequence into the box on the screen. The coin icon rotated from front to back on the screen as the room waited in silence.

Aunt Pookie commented, "Heavens to Betsy, the suspense is killing me! Did it work?"

Sam and Judy both shrieked, and Sam started jumping up and down. "It says you can access your wallet!"

Aunt Pookie turned and grabbed Edwin in a big bear hug that Sam would have rolled her eyes at if she wasn't so happy that they found the key. Sam leaned over the desk and offered up her hand to Mr. Fletcher and Aunt Pookie for a couple of high-fives.

"Mom, you did it! That is your key!"

"Yes, Sam, it is, but look at this message on my screen."

Sam went back behind her mom and leaned over her shoulder. Judy's wallet now had a green check mark beside it and a new box that instructed the user to transfer the offline stored coins back to the virtual bank website for further options in spending or monetizing the coins.

"Oh, you have got to be kidding me!" Sam yelled, "Mom, your coins were stored offline? Where?"

Mr. Fletcher cleared his throat and said, "If you are talking about cryptocurrency, your coins are generally stored on an external hard drive."

All three heads whipped around to stare at Edwin, and Sam astonishingly said, "I believe my friend, Leo, did say something about offline storage, but the website never indicated that they were stored anywhere except online in her virtual wallet. It even showed us the balance that she had in the account!"

"That may be true, Sam, but if the website is telling you to upload the coins back to your mom's account, then they are not stored on their website. All you need to do is transfer them back, and along with the key you now have, you can monetize or trade them any way that you want."

Sam hung her head, closed her eyes, and took a deep breath. "Mom, any clue as to where the coins are stored?"

Judy was still staring at her screen and said, "The only thing that makes sense to me is that they were on the old laptop."

Sam's head shot up, and she took off in a jog for her bedroom in search of her cell phone. Finding it buried in her backpack, she quickly called Nic. When he didn't answer the call, she left a frantic message for him to call her right away and to not recycle her mom's laptop. She followed that up with a text that covered the same information. Sitting on the side of her bed, biting her lower lip, and trying to figure out what she should do next, she dialed Darby.

Sam almost cried when she heard Darby answer on the first ring, "Hey friend, what's going on?"

"Darby! Do you know where Nic is? Did you tell him to get rid of that old laptop of Mom's that we were talking about at dinner the other night?"

"Sam, I did, and he said he would take care of it. What's going on?"

Sam quickly filled her friend in on what might be stored on the old laptop and that she needed to get it back from Nic right away.

"But I don't understand. If Nic told you that the laptop was trashed, how are you going to get anything off of it even if he hasn't already recycled it?"

"I'm not sure about that, but I have to at least try. Please tell Nic to call me if you talk to him soon."

Sam went back into the kitchen, where Aunt Pookie, Mr. Fletcher, and her mom were once again gathered around the kitchen table.

"Mom, your old laptop is probably gone. When Nic couldn't get it to work, I told him to get rid of it."

The room was silent, and Mr. Fletcher softly said, "Maybe the coins were not stored on the laptop."

Judy sadly said, "I don't know where else they would be, but maybe it will come back to me. The email we received did say that we could use the coins in perpetuity."

"I'm so sorry, Mom. I was just trying to help."

"Sam, there's no guarantee that the coins were even stored on that laptop. I just don't know."

Aunt Pookie finally spoke up and said, "Well, that's just as sad as a three-legged dog on a tightrope."

CHAPTER 31

The next day, Sam felt like she was working through her normal morning routine while in slow motion, and time just wouldn't move fast enough. She left another voice message for Nic, and as soon as she finished teaching her first class, she got in the Booger and headed to the local branch of the National Bank of Texas. Sam wasn't going to wait around for Mr. Wilburn to call her back. Good 'ole Charles was going to be looking into her eyeballs when she got approval from him to extend the time they had before the bank foreclosed on their home.

Hair in a high pony, aviators on, and rocking her black, faux leather leggings, she marched into the lobby of the bank and asked which office Mr. Charles Wilburn was occupying. A skinny intern with a wrinkled white shirt and a pair of dress pants that looked like he had borrowed them from his much bigger brother mutely pointed her down a hall and to a back office.

Sam silently stood at the office door and waited to be recognized, but when she realized that the occupant was not going to look up from his computer screen, she tapped politely on the metal door frame.

"Excuse me. I'm looking for Charles Wilburn."

The man sitting at his wood grain viny-wrapped desk jumped a little, and Sam thought he probably wasn't used to talking to real people because he stammered and said, "W-who let you back here? Do you have an appointment?"

"Are you Mr. Wilburn?"

"Yes, and you are?"

At this point, Sam let herself into his office and set her backpack down at her feet as she took the guest chair in front of his desk. Eyeing her suspiciously and touching the three hairs plastered across the top of his head in an unconvincing comb-over, Mr. Wilburn sat up straighter in his rolling desk chair and looked nervously at the door.

Sam pushed her sunglasses on top of her head and reached across his desk to shake his hand, saying, "Sawyer Anne Martin. I've left you a few messages."

Mr. Wilburn tentatively leaned forward, straining the buttons on his striped work shirt, and gave her a dead fish handshake, which Sam immediately took as a bad sign. True Southerners knew how important steady eye contact and a firm grip were when meeting someone new, and clearly, this man was either not following those guidelines, or not raised as a Southern gentleman. Sam opened her mouth to begin her spiel when the banker held up his hand in a stop gesture.

"Ms. Martin, I did receive your messages, but if you had only taken the time to read the foreclosure notification in its entirety, this meeting would not be necessary. The letter had all the facts pertaining to the foreclosure proceedings and the rules that we follow in these circumstances." He gently ran his fingertips over the long swooping hairs on the top of his head and finished with, "If you had read the notice, you would have known that we cannot deviate from the bank policies."

"Mr. Wilburn, if you could just give us an extra four to six weeks, we may be able to get the mortgage up to date. We've lived in that house for over twenty years, and my mom has never been late on a mortgage payment until just recently. Please, the deadline that you gave us in the notification just isn't enough time."

"I'm sorry, Ms. Martin, but maybe your time would be more wisely spent packing up your personal belongings instead of coming here without an appointment and interrupting my workday."

Sam narrowed her eyes, raised herself up to her full five feet and nine inches, and said, "Mr. Wilburn, let me tell you something. I have three speeds: on, off, and don't push your luck. If you say one more thing, you'll have me on my last speed, and you don't want to see that." She took a deep breath and then added, "My mother raised an understanding and kind person. I can see that your momma struggled with that task."

Sam picked up her backpack, slung it over her shoulder, and huffed right back to the Booger. She sat in the Jeep for a few minutes and tried to perform some deep breathing techniques to lower her blood pressure and get her thoughts under control. She checked her phone and saw that she had missed a call from Nic, but he had not left a message. Dialing him back and saying a silent prayer that he would pick up the call, she almost wanted to cry when she heard his voice.

"Hi, Sam. I'm sorry that I missed your calls."

"It's fine. Did you get my messages? Do you have my mom's laptop?"

Sam knew from the hesitation in his answer that she was not going to like his response.

"No. When we talked about recycling it and then Darby told me that you said to go ahead and dispose of it, I did just that. I'm sorry. Darby explained to me that you were hoping to retrieve some information on the hard drive."

Letting out a sigh, Sam said, "It's not your fault, Nic. You were only doing what I asked you to do, and I'm not even sure if the laptop was used to store the, um, information or not."

After hanging up with Nic, Sam took out her day planner, updated her to-do list, and checked her schedule for the rest of the day. She was giving her presentation on her marketing project in class tomorrow evening. Then, with that task completed, she would focus on getting in touch with a few home builders in the Golden Oaks and Oak Forest areas to see if they could quickly come to an agreement on the sale of the bungalow on Lamonte Lane.

Sam talked to herself all the way back to the studio, and by the time she arrived, she almost had herself convinced that everything was going to be alright. The fact that her mom's recent health issues were going to be controlled by medication and her brain fog should clear was more than she could have hoped for, and she knew she should be grateful for that alone. Having to move out of the bungalow and home that they loved and find a new place to live that they could afford, was not an ideal situation. She hoped they would get some help if she could find a willing builder to buy the property as a teardown.

Sam parked at the rear of the building and let herself in through the back office. Trying to think positively and give her clients the consideration and attentiveness that they deserved, she plastered a smile on her face and walked to the reception area to greet the next class that was starting to check in.

Dolly looked up at Sam as she wandered over to the desk and gave her a quick smile.

"Sam, I've got everything under control here, and I have your class breakdown if you would like to go over that."

"Dolly, you're doing a great job, and I want you to know that I appreciate how you have made this studio a better place to work."

Dolly beamed and shimmered in her sequined T-shirt that said, "I'm a ray of tucking sunshine!", and Sam felt bad that she hadn't said something to her sooner. Clearly, her new coworker had embraced the whole barre working experience.

CHAPTER 32

Sam got up the next morning and replayed in her head the conversation that she had had with her mom the night before. She had told Judy about her visit to the bank and Mr. Wilburn's lack of empathy or help. Sam explained that she thought that they should look for a builder who would buy the house for a teardown and a quick payout. Judy understood the financial ramifications of selling the house for what they could get, paying off the mortgage, and then having a small nest egg to live on temporarily. She also understood that she needed to get herself together and start bringing in some income, but she just wasn't sure if she wanted to go back into bean counting, as her Grammy always called her profession.

Sam grabbed her day planner and looked over her list. Today Sam was prepared to give her marketing project presentation, and then she would see if she needed to wait to enroll in her next class. It all depended on how quickly they could find a buyer, and their daily lives calmed down.

She spent extra time on her hair and makeup and sorted through her closet until she came up with a pair of professional looking navy pants and a white fitted button down blouse to change into before her presentation. There was no way Sam was going to look professional and polished in her regular leggings, sports bra, and T-shirt, but the simple navy pants and white shirt were the best that she could scrounge up. Sam packed up her backpack and her change of clothes and made it to work with time to spare.

Darby was at the desk when Sam arrived, and she felt guilt niggling at her conscience again when she thought to herself that Dolly would have had the candle lit and her class breakdown ready to review.

"Hi, friend. I talked to Nic, and he told me that the laptop was gone. I'm so sorry."

Sam sighed and said, "It's not his fault. He only did what I told him to do, and anyway, Mom's not even sure that the coins were stored on that old laptop. It was just a guess."

"So, what are y'all going to do?"

"Well, I think the best course of action is to try and get a builder to come and buy the house for a teardown. Mom could at least get some money for it, pay off the remaining mortgage, and we could move somewhere until she gets to feeling better and finds a job. I can try to finish school and work full-time."

"Sheesh, Sam, you're already running around like a chicken with its head cut off. How are you going to manage all of this? Do you have a builder in mind?"

"No, I'm going to work on that as soon as I finish my marketing class. I give my presentation in class this evening."

"At least that will be one thing you can mark off your to-do list. I don't have class today, so Nic is going to cook me dinner tonight. What do you think about that?"

"I think I'm jealous that you are going to have a nice relaxing evening with someone waiting on you hand and foot. Are you sure he's cooking, or is he ordering out and just having it delivered? I'm just saying, there is a difference."

"I hear you loud and clear, Sam, but bless his heart, he's trying to be a nice person, so I'm going to let him keep working at it," Darby said with a sly smile.

"You go, Alabama girl," and Sam headed into the studio to get ready to lead her students in a session of lifting, tucking, and pulsing at the barre.

When Sam finished her last class of the day, she hurried to the small bathroom and did what she could to look and smell presentable. This involved a lot of deodorant and some perfume to cover her sweaty work aroma. Freshening up as best she could and changing into her presentation outfit, she peeked her head out of the office door. She told Darby to wish her luck on her project, and then added in a whisper to use the sugar sparingly this evening so none of the other Bar Babes patrons would hear her.

Darby grinned, gave her a big thumbs up, and said, "You're fixin' to knock'em dead, and don't worry about the sweets, I've got him on a sugar-free diet for the time being."

Sam wasn't going to take any chances with the Houston traffic and allowed herself forty-five minutes to get to the University of Houston's downtown campus. Unfortunately, this was one of those days that, even with the best of planning, Sam knew she was going to be cutting it close. A semi-rig that was carrying a load of forty thousand pounds of avocados had slid onto its side and then caught fire at I-45 and Allen Parkway. The traffic in the downtown area was gridlocked, and the local news and traffic reporters continued yucking it up with nonstop reports that started with lead-ins like, "Holy Guacamole, traffic is going to be bad for a while!" Sam couldn't help but laugh to herself when she thought about all the Houstonians who would gladly help eliminate the roadside mess.

No stranger to these kinds of traffic snarls, Sam exited the freeway and wound through the side roads until she made it to the Vine Street garage. Speedwalking from the parking garage, Sam thought that she heard her name but continued towards the glass doors of the campus building. Rushing into the Marilyn Davies College of Business classroom, Sam selected her seat and got her presentation notes out to review. Professor Wood walked in two minutes later, gave a summary of the class presenters, and handed out evaluation papers to the rest of the class for their feedback on each project. She also brought in a plastic container of her latest batch of cookies and set them on her desk for all to sample, telling everyone to help themselves at the end of class.

Sam thanked the marketing report gods that she wasn't first on the presentation list and attempted to focus on the reports that were being given by her fellow classmates while she tried to remain calm. When it was her turn to present to the class, Sam took her notes and stood at the podium at the front of the classroom. Professor Wood only allowed an oral presentation to the class without the accompaniment of a fancy computerized presentation program. Sam's business plan and summary had already been turned in electronically, and this was the part of the project where she was supposed to sell her idea to prospective investors or partners.

Professor Wood said, "Ms. Martin, you may begin when you are ready."

Sam took a calming breath and then began with, "Good evening, my name is Sawyer Martin, and I want to thank you for taking the time to attend my presentation on the concept of a new type of barre and lifestyle training facility." She paused for a second and then tried to look into the eyes of each of her fellow students and said, "What if I told you that one in every three of you in this room right now is going to die with Alzheimer's or some other form of dementia when you become a senior citizen? Or what if I told you that over two-thirds of Americans living with Alzheimer's are women?" She then paused for a second while that information soaked in and then said, "What if I also told you that exercise, nutrition, and early intervention and testing for those who show signs of memory loss or comprehension can significantly help to delay or prolong the full onset of the disease? That is why my business plan for my company will follow a two-pronged configuration. We will offer regular barre classes along with lifestyle and nutritional guidance to my clients, but I also propose a division that will be a community outreach and service sector. In this part of my business plan, I propose to offer classes to individuals with early to middle stages of dementia. These classes will incorporate the affected individual's caregiver and be a more general, fluid class with music, dancing, and gentle movements that the clients could replicate."

Sam looked over at Professor Wood and saw that she was nodding her head, and Sam knew that she had accomplished what her teacher had told her to do with her project—to find something that she was passionate about. After the last couple of months, Sam's eyes had been opened to the magnitude of a dementia diagnosis and how it affects the entire family. In Sam's case, she had the support of her aunts, uncles, and cousins, but she knew that the main responsibility of caring for her mother would always fall on her shoulders, whether it was dementia or some other physical ailment in her future. Sam just knew that luck had nothing to do with her mom having a treatable thyroid condition, but it was most assuredly the result of a good doctor, early intervention, and the good Lord above.

When she was finished with the financial data section of her presentation, she concluded with her idea to add to the community outreach part of the business by hosting the occasional pop-up class at some of the memory care live-in facilities that were in the Houston area. It would be Sam's waying of giving back to the community she had called home for her entire life.

Thanking everyone for their time and attention, Sam moved back to her desk and relaxed as she felt like a huge weight had been lifted from her shoulders. She also felt good that her dream of owning and running a barre studio now had the added distinction of serving and assisting families that were dealing with dementia.

Feeling relieved, Sam felt lighter and happier than she had for weeks. Not being able to find the coins from her mom's savings account was not ideal, but it wasn't going to be the end of the world. Her mom had her health and her mind, and that was something to celebrate. Sam would make sure that they looked at their upcoming move as an adventure and a fun new chapter in both of their lives.

At the end of class, Sam was gathering her things and had her evaluation papers to turn in to the teacher when the cardigan-clad Professor Wood walked over to where Sam was seated.

"Ms. Martin, I enjoyed your presentation and your realization about how important it is to give back to the community, no matter what type of business you are trying to establish. Also, your idea for classes for memory-impaired clients touched me personally because my father had dementia, and it's a very cruel disease to experience with a loved one. Excellent job."

Sam thanked her and handed her the evaluation papers she had in her hand from the other presentations that had taken place that evening. Taking her time and exiting the classroom when she finally had everything stowed back in her backpack and a fresh cookie in her hand, she was surprised to see Becca and Roadkill leaning against the wall across the hall from her class.

Becca, straight-faced and unemotional as ever, stared at the cookie in her hand and commented, "What is this, a home economics class?"

Not knowing why she felt so intimidated by the IT duo, Sam quickly dropped the cookie in her backpack and said, "Um, no, no, my professor just likes to bake. She's really, um, sweet." Nervously laughing, she said, "Get it?"

Both computer geeks just stared at her blankly.

"Anyway, it's good seeing you both, but I need to run. Is there something I can help y'all with?"

Roadkill spoke softly and said, "Becca was taking apart your laptop to recycle it, and she came across an M.2 SSD when she removed the lower clamshell. The processing unit and the original hard drive are shot, but we thought you might want the SSD."

Sam stared alarmed at both IT students and stuttered, "Wait a minute, I don't know what that means. It almost sounds like you're saying Mom's laptop has a, um, disease?"

Becca casually reached into her back pocket and held up a sealed baggie with a tiny computer piece inside.

Roadkill and Becca glanced at each other and did their silent mind-meld communication where Sam was sure they were saying, *"Can you believe this lower-level species is so clueless? Let's talk slowly to her."*

Becca put the bag in Sam's hand and said, "It's a type of storage device that contains non-volatile flash memory. An SSD, not an STD."

Sam just stood there holding the baggie and staring at the pair. Slowly, her thoughts started to come together, and she finally asked them, "Are you saying that this little piece of equipment is storage from my mom's computer and there is something stored on here?"

Becca opened her mouth to answer when Roadkill held up his hand and simply said, "We couldn't access it on the old laptop because it was fried, but if you attach it to a working computer, it is possible that you could access what's on it."

Sam held the baggie to her chest and cried, "Oh my goodness, you have no idea how big this could be! Thank you! Thank you! Thank you!"

Becca's face finally cracked a small smile and said, "Any friend of Nic's is a friend of ours. Happy we could help."

Sam grinned and said, "Well, you are one smart cookie! Get it?"

Becca slowly shook her head back and forth, and the geeky pair turned and walked away.

CHAPTER 33

Rushing as fast as she could to the Booger and clutching the baggie with the computer SSD in her one hand, Sam fumbled in her backpack to find her phone. Reaching the parking garage and finally finding her phone, which was now liberally coated in crushed sugar cookie remnants, she called Darby.

When the line was answered and before Darby could even say hello, Sam was shrieking on the phone, "Darby, Darby, I need to see Nic! Right now!"

"Whoa, girl. What's the problem?"

"His friends, the geek twins, found something on Mom's laptop! I need him to come to the house right now and look at it! Please!"

"Calm down. I'll have Wolfgang Puck here turn everything off that he has cooking, and we'll meet you at the house."

"Darby, I'm sorry about interrupting your dinner, but this could be really important!"

"Hell's bells, Sam, don't worry about dinner. I can be waited on any ol' day, and I'd like to know what was found, too."

Sam sent a quick text to her mom, telling her that Darby and Nic would be coming to the house soon and that she was headed home as well. Not waiting to see if she got a response, Sam drove towards the GOOF area as fast as she dared push the Booger and the speed limits. Trying to piece everything together, she thought that it made sense to her that if the computer was equipped with this separate storage drive, maybe that's where the MoneyTreeCoins were held. Promising herself that she needed to learn a little bit more than just the basics about computers, as in power on and power off, Sam made a mental note to add that to her ongoing to-do list.

When she finally turned onto Lamonte Lane and the peeling little bungalow came into view, she could see that Aunt Pookie's Mini-Cooper with the eye-lashed headlights and Nic's smart little red Audi were parked on the street in front of the house. The Booger took the driveway on what felt like two wheels, and Sam barely had the Jeep in park before running towards the front door. Before she made it all the way there, the door opened, and Judy, Aunt Pookie, Darby, and Nic were all staring at her as she held the baggie up yelling, "This may be the coins! The geek gang found it on Mom's old laptop. Try not to get too excited, but this *may be the coins!*"

Judy stepped forward from the group and said, "Sam, dear, we are all calm. It's you that's having a dying duck fit."

Sam slowed down and held the baggie up to Nic. "Do you think this could be something? Could this little thing hold cryptocurrency?"

Nic took the baggie from Sam and started slowly looking it over from front to back. "Possibly. This is an after-market storage device that someone must have added to the laptop after it was purchased. There's only one way to find out what it holds, and that's to reinstall it on a working computer."

Aunt Pookie, who had been shockingly quiet, held up her hand like she was the gesticulating Queen of England, and motioned for everyone to follow her towards the office. Nic assumed a position behind the desk, lifted the tower, and placed it on the tabletop. He turned it off, unplugged it from the power, and then removed all the cables. After a few frantic minutes of trying to find a small enough screwdriver to remove the side panel retaining screws, he finally got access to the inside of the computer and went to work.

The four women all stood uncommonly quiet watching Nic try to reinstall the little storage piece. Sam looked over at her mom, who was literally wringing her hands in front of her and reached over and grabbed one. Judy looked at her and gave her a soft smile, and Sam said, "If this doesn't work and the coins are not there, we are still going to be okay."

"You're right, dear, but I just wish I could recall where they are or what I did with them. I didn't even know that that little device was on my old worktop. I guess Bill could have done that when he set all of this up."

Nic started the process of putting the desktop components back together and plugging them all back into the monitor, keyboard, and mouse. The entire room was holding their collective breath when Nic finally pushed the power button, and the workstation came back to life.

Pookie finally broke the silence and blurted, "My dear, I can see that this isn't your first rodeo from the way you wrangled that computer, but for heaven's sake, please tell us that you can see what's on that little doodad."

Nic finally looked up and grinned at his audience. "It's installed and recognized as a new working component."

The ladies all whooped and pumped their fists, and then Sam went and stood behind Nic. "Now what do we do?"

"My suggestion is that you log into your online account and let's see if we can get the site to interpret what is stored on the SSD."

Nic and Sam stood back, and Judy walked forward and took a seat behind the desk. She logged into her account and once again clicked on her wallet icon, where she was prompted to enter her personal identity key. Sam retrieved the Rolodex card and slowly read off the nineteen-digit code, "S-A-M-0-5-2-1-1-9-9-4-1-1-3-4-2-0-0-9."

Darby whispered to Aunt Pookie, "I get the S-A-M part of the code, but what does the rest of it mean?"

Pookie said, "It is quite simple if you think about it. Sam's birthday is May 21, 1994, so that's the 0-5-2-1-1-9-9-4. The next four digits are the address of this house, 1134, and 2009, I bet, is the year that Judy opened the MoneyTreeCoins account."

Darby nodded her head and said, "Well, my stars, that's the perfect code."

The wallet icon finally turned green and prompted Judy to transfer the offline coins back to her account. Nervously, with Nic's guidance, Judy clicked the search button to direct the site where to find the coins and let out a gasp when the new SSD was recognized as a viable option. Clicking on the storage device, the computer immediately started whirling, and an onscreen timer started counting toward the completion of an acceptable upload.

Sam grasped one of her mother's shoulders and had a death grip on Nic's arm when the sound of leaves rustling in the wind and a bell came from the computer, along with a notification that said:

Your MoneyTreeCoins are available to use in your wallet.

"Mom, you did it! It's your savings account!"

Tears and hugs came from everyone in the room. Aunt Pookie was dancing a little jig in the den, and Judy left her desk seat to join her in her celebration. Sam looked over as Darby was hugging Nic, who was looking quite pleased with himself. She turned to Sam and said, "He may think the sun comes up just to hear him crow, but I'm starting to think it's true as well."

"Nic, thank you so much. You have no idea what this means to us."

Winking at Sam, and gesturing with his head towards Judy, he said, "I'm happy she's in the millionaire's club."

Sam smirked and said, "Well, I don't know about the *club*, and it's not quite a million dollars, but it's more than enough to make a difference in Mom's life."

EPILOGUE

Sam got home from the studio a week after finding the offline coins and was excited to see the work crews at the house on Lamonte Lane. There were men on the roof tearing off the old shingles and throwing them to the ground, and there was also a crew replacing some of the rotting wood around the windows and the eaves in preparation for the new paint job.

Sam had finally seen a sample of the paint colors that were selected by her mother and approved by GOMO, and she was pleasantly surprised that the main color of the house was a soft yellow. However, the accent color for the shutters, windows, and doors was a bright green that bordered on the fluorescent spectrum. She promised herself that she would smile and nod appreciatively if she was asked about the color combination.

Sam realized that a certain individual had to intervene to get the final approval from the homeowner's association for that particular accent shade. She was grateful for his ongoing help, and even now, Mr. Fletcher stood in the front yard and was vigilantly watching every move that the workers were making.

Sam parked the Booger and went over to join him in the front yard.

"Mr. Fletcher, thank you so much for getting us the contractors that we needed to start the work on our house."

He turned in his overalls and said, "Sam, I've told you all along that I'm happy to help. Um, by the way, is Pookie going to be around anytime soon?"

Sam held in an ewwwww, and her mind was spinning as she thought about poor Dolly and said, "Hmm. I'll have to get back to you on that. Thanks again for all your help!"

Walking into the house, she found her mom, in the kitchen starting a new batch of kolaches.

"Who is this batch for, Mom?"

"I'm just tweaking my recipe and writing all this down. I also thought I would give some to all the workers here at the house."

"That's very nice of you."

Judy looked a little sheepish and then said, "I've been thinking, Sam. Maybe what I will do is open my own kolache shop. It's something that I have always loved to do, and I'm ready for a career change and a new chapter in my life. What do you think?"

Sam smiled at her mom and answered, "Now that you're in high cotton, as Grammy used to say, I think you should go for it."

"Oh, I would never use all my savings to open the kolache shop. I'm going to be smart about my retirement money. In fact, I called Leo and asked him to come over later to help me with a more stable portfolio."

Sam's head whipped up, and she said, "Leo's coming here? Tonight?"

Judy smiled and said, "Why, yes, he is, dear. Maybe you should go shower and change?"

Sam smiled to herself and thought, *You are exactly right. I do need to shower and change because I believe he may need to borrow a little sugar.*

ACKNOWLEDGEMENT

This book is something that I was motivated to write to unite with and support the dementia community and to validate and praise those individuals who work tirelessly as caregivers. This disease is as unprejudiced as it is relentless as it consumes your loved one. I have traveled this road once with my father, and now again with my dear mother.

I need to thank my three sisters, Christina, Caren, and Catherine, for their continual love, support, care, and patience in taking care of Dad, and now Mom. It is truly a group effort.

An incredibly special thank you to Carrie Aalberts, the Dementia Darling, for so kindly agreeing to write the introduction. Her guidance, suggestions, and encouragement to caregivers are enlightening and refreshing. Please take the opportunity to connect with her on her website, www.dementiadarling.com.

Cheers to Jane Anniboli, Karen Brennan, and Cara Mason for your input and suggestions as my beta readers. Thank you for keeping me headed in the right direction.

To my family, Derek, Cara, Nic, Troop, Sawyer, Mallory, Kyle, Mack, Haylee, Charlie, and Buc, you are my world.